"Sheila Kaye-Smith's English is exquisite . . . This book can surely rank as a great Catholic novel." *Best Sellers*

"Thrilling romance . . . Laughter and love and blood and fire and mob fury whirl through it." *Commonweal*

"Taut and tense in the telling. Perhaps *Superstition Corner* is tinged with melodrama. But the theme and the story never droop or lag or dip into the saccharine. It is charged with the energy of faith under siege. Here, alive and glowing, are the alternating fear and courage, anxiety and elation of the loyal Catholic who dared to resist the Established Church under Elizabeth I. Truly *Superstition Corner* is a book to live." *Books On Trial*

"Only a writer who is at once a realist and a mystic could have worked this special miracle for us." New York *Times*

"Miss Kaye-Smith presents her Kate so candidly and with such clarity and understanding that the reader unconsciously develops the same fondness and pity for her which her creator also feels but artfully hides. The book is beautifully written, its proportions are just, its key beautifully maintained." *Books*

"What a fresh, vigorous tale it is . . . 'Galloping Kate', Master Pecksall, the renegade priest, and the Alard family are all characterized with masterly brevity and force. *Superstition Corner* is a book that looks both forward and back, and in so doing it provides excitement and rare insight." *Catholic World*

D1252905

Superstition Corner

Sheila Kaye-Smith

Preface by G. B. Stern

Image Books

A Division of Doubleday & Company, Inc.
Garden City, New York

Typography by Edward Gorey

Image Books edition 1958
by special arrangement with Harper & Brothers

Image Books edition published February 1958
1st printing...........December 1957

A selection of the Catholic Book Club, May 1934
A selection of the Thomas More Book Club, February 1955
A selection of Catholic Family Book Club, January 1957

A Thomas More Book To Live

Preface

WHEN SHEILA KAYE-SMITH is asked to name her favorite among her books, she invariably replies: "The one I'm writing now—otherwise I couldn't write it." This is how it should be with an author; that she writes a book for no ulterior motives, but because it *has* to be written, because she is dedicated to her theme until it has been safely delivered; so possessed by it that all her former work, its conception and reception, is meanwhile entirely forgotten. Perhaps in the sense of being enamoured by the sacrament of the present book in the same way that Cardinal Newman meant when he talked of the "Sacrament of the present moment," her very bones are informed with the desire to make just this one piece of truth articulate. Nevertheless, to account for her large and enthusiastic public, it must be insisted that she writes real "storybooks," free from any tendency towards what is horridly known as moral uplift; thus placing her among that little band of modern writers who are helping to restore to their original intention so many words which once functioned as crusaders for God and the Saints, but have since acquired priggish and even hypocritical associations; words such as sanctity, saintly, religious, holy, and a hundred others; deterioration which can be easily recognized and put among Satan's more successful side-lines.

As well as being a "teller of tales," Miss Kaye-Smith has a pleasing ironic humor, of which an instance appears at the very start of *Superstition Corner*, where Queen Elizabeth Tudor's soldiers, "their hearts gay and childlike in the hope of destruction," destroy the stone cross that had been standing for countless years on the crossways at Holy Horns. Her beloved Jane Austen used the same slant of irony, leaving the laugh to the reader's quick collaboration; though in many

5

other ways, such as her gusto and earthiness, Sheila Kaye-Smith's work derives rather from the eighteenth-century novelists whom she devoured when she was very young: Smollett, Richardson, Sterne, Fielding.

The heroine of *Superstition Corner*, young Mistress Catherine Alard ("galloping Kate" the yokels called her, for her love of wild riding) has little affinity with the ways of the sweet and delicate heroine clinging to a sturdy male hero, which has come to be linked with old-fashioned historical fiction. Sheila Kaye-Smith was brought up by the kindest of parents, her childhood sheltered as a matter of course from any unorthodox or rumbustious elements. Yet "banquets do not always tempt those who are used to eating under hedges," and from her very first book—*The Tramping Methodist*—she has always revealed a huge scorn of any form of daintiness; longing to have been herself a rebel and a tomboy, she found comfort, therefore, in the endowment of her book heroines with just these thrilling traits: "Galloping Kate" she says, had all her life been "a gipsy in religion," reminding us indeed, as her author intended, of one of those valiant Shakespearean maidens who dressed as a boy when the need arose for a display of desperate courage unhampered by feminine apparel:

> "She examined her brother's clothes . . . they would doubtless fit her well. . . . It seemed delightful and strange to be no longer kicking at the folds of a great skirt."

—echo of Viola, not Ophelia; of Rosalind and Imogen, with Desdemona impatiently discarded. And *Superstition Corner* is laid in Shakespeare's own day.

Apart from its portrait of Kate, it contains other recognizable ingredients of a first-class Sheila Kaye-Smith novel; the bitter conflict between love and conscience, men and women locked in a struggle where often the outcome had to be suffering and death for the nobler of the protagonists; and her passion for Sussex farming and the soil. It belongs, roughly speaking, to her middle period, recalling that even in extreme youth she had never thrown in her lot with the group of very young writers who shared a prevailing delight in the quaint and whimsical; on the contrary, she revelled in exaggerated violence, grim fighting and the horrors of religious persecu-

6

tion, all depicted quite without deference to the reader's nerves.

The persecution of Catholics in England resembles in many ways the persecution of the first Christians in Rome. Both lasted for about three hundred years, during which comparatively quiet intervals of merely legal prescription alternated with outbreaks of almost maniacal violence. It was such outbreaks that gave the Church in England, like the Early Church, its rich crop of martyrs, and one of them—that following the defeat of the Spanish Armada in 1588—is the time setting of *Superstition Corner*. The scene of martyrdom at Chichester is only partly fiction.

Sheila Kaye-Smith's constant return to Sussex as a setting for her stories should not, however, create an idea that they are of purely "local" interest because attached specifically to a county of England; paradoxically, we can say that they are the more universal: for in America, France, all over the world, we find this mysterious preference, usually by birth or by blood-heritage, for one small familiar spot—a farm, a house, a field; we have only to transpose the actual name, and the emotion remains universal in time and place. . . . Where the Lord has planted us in a small corner, He has also made us free of compassionate catholicity with all mankind. Von Hügel remarked once that could he only know a daisy, really *know* it, he would know everything. And perhaps, in our present context, by really knowing Sussex, Sheila Kaye-Smith can take us traveling to the utmost limits of the cosmos, North, South, East and West, the same firmament over all. And this Kate of *Superstition Corner*, especially, cannot be separated from the firmament; in modern parlance, she had a firmament fixation; even when in the physical throes of her pathetic longing to be wooed by her mother's illicit lover, still she could not wholly wrench herself from the pull of an earlier Claimant—

"The Lord became my protector and he brought me forth into a large place . . . the Lord is my firmament, and my refuge, and my deliverer."

At this juncture, lest the would-be readers imagine they will get too much firmament in this generous spread—(do you remember, in the negro play of *Green Pastures*, how de Lawd

7

and de Custard Maker enjoyed spooning up great bowls of "de firmament"?)—we will quote as companion piece from Oliver and Maria's riotous wedding feast at Holly Crouch, where Catherine confessed:

> "I was all lumperdee clumperdee after the eel pie. I'm uncommon fond of eel pie, and maybe I ate too much of it. I'm light again now."

The chapter, too, of the little astrologer's fortune-telling at Conster Manor is one of the most vivid in the book, a delightful weaving of authentic belief in the conjunction of the stars, with superstition, fear, fine promises, mumbo-jumbo—and a sudden outburst in despite of expedience: "Simon Alard goes to the Crusades, and rides against the true religion. His sister rides to meet him, and they meet under the Cross. . . ." The Squire, Kate's father, swears "By Mary-gipsy!" that he believed the man to be a mountebank, and adds in the same breath: "but I'm uncommon glad he told me such a fine fortune!"

It need not be supposed that all or even most of Miss Kaye-Smith's books are on directly Catholic themes; she has a wide range; and if we look at the long list of her novels which she has been writing for nearly fifty years without any noticeable diminution of intent or power, one may be inclined to agree with a remark made by Mr. Somerset Maugham, that on general lines it is quantity no less than quality in an author's output which should earn them professional status and a growing confidence of their readers that, unlike what happens when one showy *tour de force* is followed by an inexplicable silence while the author lazily waits for further inspiration, here they can rely on steady service and a conviction of the living truth evident in human behaviour under stress, whether the characters assembled be on the side of the Angels or under the plausible leadership of the Devil.

G. B. STERN

Chapter One

THE ROAD from Vinehall meets the road from Leasan at Superstition Corner. A few yards farther on, the London road runs off westward through Harlot's Wood, while the road to Hastings winds southward down the hill, past Newhouse and Doucegrove, deep into the valley of the River Tillingham.

Long ago, before Newhouse and Doucegrove were built, when Harlot's Wood was Haneholt's Wood, and the Forest of Medyrsham met the Forest of Wogenmarye down by the ford across the Tillingham, Superstition Corner was known as Holly or Holy Horns, because of the long corners of land that ran out into the crossways, and because of the big stone cross that stood facing northward from the edge of Dodyland Shaw. No one knew when the cross was built or who had set it up, but its tradition went back for many hundred years and it had given its name to the farmstead of Holly Crouch Yard, already so old that it was crumbling into decay.

One summer evening a little party of soldiers came riding up from Leasan towards the throws. They carried crowbars and iron-tipped staves, which they had taken from the smithy, and their hearts were gay and childlike with the hope of destruction. It had been a rare piece of luck to hear that there was a fine, tall, superstitious cross standing in the neighbourhood and crying out to be cast down. Riding among the villages, they had found that most survivals of Popery had already disappeared; it seemed a marvel that this one had not been overthrown. Doubtless it was because Kent and Sussex were more ignorant and wild than other parts; perhaps the common folk did not yet know they were Protestants. They might as well learn it to-day, with the smoke of the Hastings beacon fires still drifting with the evening fogs over Odimere Ridge, to tell them that the King of Spain had been harried into Calais harbour and harried out again, and was now scattering his power into the north, routed by the fire-ships of Francis Drake and the sou'-west wind of God.

The cross-roads lay empty. Neither man nor beast trod the hard yellow ruts of the four wentways, and the long, unfenced corners of land, rank with coarse grass and sour with thistles, pastured neither goat nor hog. The only dwelling near was Holly Crouch, and that was hidden away behind Dodyland Shaw. The soldiers were scarcely pleased to have no spectators; the rioting crowds that had tried to protect their idols in the first years of destruction would not be unwelcome now. But even when they smote the monument with their crowbars and shouted at it in their religious zeal, none answered but a faint echo from the shaw, and the sighing rush of the wind whose mainguard on the seas was driving King Philip to the Orkneys.

The cross was soon a headless shaft.

> "Sing ho! for Headless Cross!
> Down there, beneath that tree,
> My mother cradled me . . ."

sang one of the soldiers sentimentally, while the others smote the shaft into a stump. The stones were old, and cracked and crumbled easily. The soldiers' work was soon done. They were disheartened because no one had tried to stop them.

"This is no-man's land. The idol hath eaten up his worshippers like Bel."

"By Zembletee! Better be off at once and find a lodging. I've had enough of sleeping in ditches."

"And of drinking ditchwater. To-night we'll drink lambswool and sleep in beds—the King of Spain will not land to-night."

"Nor to-morrow night, by Mack! nor any night this year nor any year. We can go back to our wives."

"Hooray!" cried some; "Cuckoo!" cried others, and they all rode off towards Vinehall, singing an old song that soon would die:

> "Com'st thou not from Walsingham?
> That holy land . . ."

2

They would no doubt have attracted more attention had the men at Holly Crouch Yard been working as usual in the fields. But as it happened, everyone to-day was busy with the new house that Thomas Harman of Holly Crouch was building for his eldest son Oliver, down at the south-west horn of his land, beside the Hastings road. Young Oliver was to be married at the end of the month, and if everyone did not work hard his house would not be ready for him. There was a clear week now before harvest, and it seemed a good opportunity for the whole farm to set to the building: all except old William Luck, of course, who was past his work, though they still kept him on the farm, since he had worked from childhood for Thomas Harman and his father.

Old William Luck sat under the hedge of Dodyland Shaw, and watched the new house a-building. His master had cut the wood out of the shaw some time ago, and for years had kept it seasoning. He had always meant to build a new house when one of his sons should marry. Old Holly Crouch was falling down, though great beams propped its leaning frontage. It had been built in the same way as the new house, of oak and a plaster mixed of sand and clay, but it was thatched instead of tiled, and its great moss-grown hump of roof had so sagged and slumped over the beams that gable-end and roof-tree were lost in it together, a shapeless mass.

William Luck was sorry that the new house was to be roofed with tiles. Slab-castles, they were called, those little tiled houses that folk were building now, and sensible men made mock of them. Tiles were all very well for the gentry, for the Squire at Conster Manor or even for the Squire at Fuggesbroke, but they weighed down the beams of small houses, making walls bulge and rafters sag—and no one could say that tiles were snug, warm in winter and cool in summer, like thatch; nor were they so easily come by as thatch, which grows in the fields as part of the gift of corn.

He was sorry that his master would not walk in the old ways his father had trodden. They were good, the old ways, and the new ways were bad, and he would always say so. In the good old days when he was a boy, folk lived quiet and contented, and when they died there was the priest to bury them. There were no priests now—they had all turned into preachers, and he did not hold with preachers any more than he held with tiles. Many and many years it was since he had seen the holy pyx hanging like a dove from the roof of Leasan

Church, or heard the good words uttered; and none of the young folk could say a paternoster—there was no use telling him Our Father was the same, because he knew different. And now they'd brought the King of Spain over and had had a hard to-do to get him away; they never had any trouble with the King of Spain in good King Harry's time.

"Whoo-oop!"

The crashing of twigs and branches in the shaw suddenly reached his deaf ears. At the same instant came a shout, and then a whirlwind passed over him, his heavens darkened with a horse's belly and his earth rocked with a horse's hoofs. "Oh, Maria! Oh, Neptune!" he cried as he sank into the ditch.

Then, as the stinging-nettles told him he was alive, fear turned to rage. Who had come charging over him like this, galloping through the shaw and leaping the hedge without looking to see if there was a Christian man behind it? Indeed, he might have guessed—that was mistress Catherine Alard galloping her horse as if the devil and all his imps rode at her crupper. He watched her go down the heathery-slope towards the farmstead, rolling in the saddle like a boy. She was a wild piece, and no man would marry her. Folk said that she must be twenty-eight—an old maid turning sour; yet she seemed more man than maid, with her loud whooping voice and her galloping ways. Folk said that she was wild for the old religion and would go crazy for the want of it: folk said she was sorry that the King of Spain's ships had been driven away.

3

But this was unjust to Catherine Alard, who felt as thankful as anyone that the Grand Armada had been defeated. Indeed, she had just ridden over to Staple Hill to see if the bonfire there was still burning: last night they had missed its red glow in the sky. She had ridden a roundabout way, and it was not till her journey home that she saw what had happened at Holly Horns. Suddenly lifting her eyes to greet the loved, familiar landmark and lifting her hand to make the sign of it on her breast, she had seen a gap and a desolation. On the slope outside the shaw lay strewn the broken stones that told their tale. Someone had thrown down the cross.

She must find out who had done it, though she knew that sacrilege was not a crime that could be punished in the land to-day. So she went charging recklessly through the shaw, set only on coming the quickest way to Holly Crouch, leaping the fence, unaware of the commotion in the ditch. The farmstead seemed deserted, but she could see a crowd of men and lads at work on the new house beside the road.

Ned Harman saw her coming. Being the youngest, he had been given the plaster to mix—beating up the fine calf's hair, mixing the sand and clay, and then when it was all set, breaking it up to powder and mixing it again.

"Look, Father! Here comes galloping Kate."

That was how they called her among themselves in the country round Holly Horns, for she always seemed to be on horseback, madding about the lanes and commons, instead of sitting in the *privée* parlour at Conster Manor with her needle or her lute, or riding out hawking or hunting with her father the Squire. Some said it was all for want of being married at the right time and of there being no nunnery left to put her in with others like her.

Thomas Harman came forward and greeted her respectfully, for she was the Manor's daughter, though she looked as wild as Queen Mab. But she seemed hardly to notice his greeting.

"Have you seen? The cross is broken down."

"Which cross?"

"Up at the Horns. 'Tis all thrown down in pieces."

There was a general exclamation of dismay from those standing by. It was many years since the cross had meant anything to them, and to the young people it was no more than a landmark. But as a landmark they held it in affection, old and young; all their lives they had seen it standing there at Holly Horns, and knew that it had stood for countless lives before them. No one had any right to throw it down, for it stood on Holly Crouch land and was part of its yeoman pride.

"Who can have done it?" cried Harman. "It 'ud need strength to break up that cross, and cold iron, too."

"Surelye, we should have heard the noise of un," said a labourer.

"It was there this morning," said Ned. "I saw it on my way to Colespore."

"It an't there now," cried Catherine Alard.

She still sat her horse—astride, for she had not yet learned the new way of riding side-saddle. Her heavy skirts spread on the horse's flank, gathered thickly at her firm young waist. Above the waist her figure was almost as spare as a boy's, though there was a feminine fullness about the throat, rising sunburned above her snow-white partlet. She carried her head high, and as she wore no hat the sun had bronzed her face to the colour of dark honey. There was another contrast of white in her teeth: she had a large mouth, and showed them grandly. Her eyes were large too, and slightly prominent, giving her rather a wild look. Her hair should have been the same colour as her eyes, nut brown, but the sun had bleached it to a shade slightly fairer than her face.

"Poor girl! she hath no breasts," thought Maria Douce, strolling up on her lover's arm. She and Oliver Harman had been the only idle couple in the yard, sitting side by side on the trunk of a felled tree and watching their house go up. Now he had brought her to greet Mistress Catherine, of whom he had often spoken, but whom she had never seen.

Oliver presented her:

"Mistress Catherine, here's Maria Douce. Her father hath left her with us while he's at Conster with Squire Alard."

"Aye, my father's mad and hath made up his mind to starve us all by blowing a furnace." Then she smiled kindly at Maria. "I'm uncommon glad to see you, for I've been told that you're as beautiful as the Queen."

Maria looked pleased. Strictly speaking, she was not beautiful, and being French she knew it; but she also knew she had a grace these hulking, shapeless Englishwomen lacked, and she was glad to have it seen. Oliver looked pleased too, and grinned all over his broad face.

"Noll," said Harman, "Mistress Catherine tells us that the cross at the Horns is broken down."

"Broken down! Who'd have dared? . . ."

"Aye, that's what we all would know. I wonder we never heard its being done."

" 'Tis a rascal shame," cried Oliver, and clenched his hand on Maria's little fist till she squealed. "Forgive me, coney bird, but that cross hath stood as long as Holly Crouch."

Catherine was pleased to see him so angry.

"If we'd but known, we could have saved it. Here we all

are like a troop, with spades and staves . . . even now maybe we could fall in with the rogues if we went after 'em."

But Thomas Harman was not inclined for that.

"We'd only get a pike through our belly or be carried off to Lob's pound. . . . No, no, Madam Kate. I'm grieved the cross is gone, but as 'tis gone I'm glad we knew nothing of it till it was too late to meddle."

"Shame on you!" cried Catherine.

"No shame at all. If we'd meddled we should all have been marked as Pope's men."

"And where's the harm of that?"

Old Thomas Harman waved his arm towards Odimere Ridge, still smoky with beacon fires.

"The harm is on the sea—driving north'ard, praise God!"

"But the Pope never sent the King of Spain."

"Never sent him! Why, folk say that he's himself on board," cried Oliver.

"Nay, the Pope would never leave Rome."

"If he's left Rome," said young Ned, "he'll par-break valiantly before he's home again."

They all laughed, except Catherine. She did not believe that the Pope had sailed with the Armada, but she could not prove it to anyone. Maria Douce looked at her unkindly and whispered something in her sweetheart's ear.

"Hush, child," he answered and led her away.

4

Catherine looked after them.

"She's an uncommon pretty piece," she said, her voice lagging, as if heavy with a thought beyond her words.

"Aye, and she brings a fortune. Her father 'ull give her five hundred pounds."

"Then it ain't true, this tale he tells of being ruined by the Catholics in France?"

"Reckon 'tis true enough, but he hath prospered in our country, like most of his kind. He's master of the Furnace at Panyngridge, and 'tis said he hath gotten bags of gold out of Sir Philip Sidney."

"And most like he'll get more out of my father."

"Most like. They can ask anything, I believe, these Frenchmen, for teaching their ways to the ironmasters. I know little about iron, but I understand that the French have a new way of smelting it, and a man who can teach that is paid all he asks."

"I'm sorry for it. I hate to see a pack of superstitious foreigners coming over here to teach heresy and pouch our money: they say the Huguenots 'ull end by having all the woollen trade at Rye, and the townsfolk are crying out to have 'em stopped."

"Surelye, I've heard the same. 'Tis a mercy they don't take to farming, since everything they do is done better than by other folk."

"I reckon if they all settle here and build houses our country 'ull be petty France. A pox on 'em! . . . But I won't stay talking of such things. I mun get home to my supper."

Harman looked round him quickly. Ned and the farm men had gone back to their work, and he and Catherine were alone together at the corner of the house.

"May I turn another word on you, Madam Kate?"

"Surelye. What is it?"

"I'd would know when next there's to be Mass at Squire Tuktone's."

Catherine stiffened in her saddle and looked at him uneasily.

"And how think you I could tell that?"

"You go there, Mistress—that's well known in all this country."

"I go there! . . . so, maybe I do. But why should you go there? You conform."

"Aye, I conform, not having a pocket for recusancy; but my heart's where it ever was."

"And how long is it since your feet went with your heart?"

"Not since Master Pecksall said Mass in Leasan Church I dunnamany years ago. I wouldn't go to Fuggesbroke . . . those Mission priests hold their lives cheaper than what I hold mine."

"Then why would you hear Mass at Fuggesbroke?"

"Because I'm growing old—sixty-nine at Christmas—and for these last months I've had a pain in my umbles that waxes with the moon. I'd fain hear Holy Mass again before I die, and go to heaven when I'm dead. I'm scared of dying in this new religion, for I'm persuaded there an't no heaven in it.

16

Maybe when I was younger I grew careless, and so long as I went to church cared not much what was done there; but when you grow old, Mistress Catherine, the shadows fall and you begin to want to see beyond them."

Catherine nodded gravely.

"Aye, and before you grow old. Those shadows at whiles trouble me too, Master, and I would that we had more light. Even in the faith there's darkness, seeing that we get our religion scarce more than once a twelvemonth. 'Tis a full twelve-month now since Mass was said at Fuggesbroke."

"Then I reckon 'tis time that a priest came again."

"Maybe one 'ull come soon. But Mistress Tuktone will make a fine coil about his reconciling you. She's scared when folks come from without. When old goody Brown came last year from Piramannys Garden she was half out of her wits, making sure the goody was a spy and would sell us all like Judas."

"Mistress Tuktone knows I ain't no spy, and if she don't, the Squire knows it, and he will speak for me."

"I'll speak for you too. I'll ride over to Fuggesbroke to-mor-row and tell 'em you wish to be reconciled. They may know when a priest is to come again . . . But not a word of it here— not even to your good wife."

"No, I shan't tell a soul till 'tis all done. My young folk are hot against the Pope's religion, all the more since this af-fair with Spain. But you mun speak for me, Mistress Kate, and tell 'em I've always been a Catholic at heart, and 'ud sooner die according to my heart than according to Master Pecksall's new book. But I pray that priest don't tarry much longer or maybe I shan't be allowed to wait for him."

"You look hale for a sick man."

"My cheeks look red because my hairs are white, and any-way you may keep rotten goods in a sound box. My outside's brave enough, but my inside's full of bots and poisons, com-bustions and cockolorums; sometimes I can scarce sleep at night for all the rousabout there is, and tur'ble pains getting me in the lunary parts."

"Have you taken nothing for it—nor seen a physician?"

"Aye, but all our physicians now are set on blood instead of broths. They pour out of us instead of pouring into us, and I'm scared to lose my blood. So I send for goody Lumsden and she makes me broths of poke-root and moonwort. But 'tis all to no purpose. Reckon 'tis in my stars that I mun die, and at my age I wouldn't mutter if I was sure of two things— that I'd die without pain and with a priest."

"I'll see that you die with a priest, Master Harman. All you have to do is to keep alive till I find one."

Her face darkened with an anxious thought. Then suddenly it grew light.

"So, Master—what if some fine day my brother came here and said Mass for us?"

"That would be indeed a fine day, Mistress, for me and for you. I ain't so sure if it would be a fine day for him."

" 'Tis five years since he went to Rome. He mun soon be coming back."

"Don't you never hear from him?"

She shook her head.

"He daren't write. It wouldn't be safe, and I've begged him not to try it. It was a Father Polydore Plasden brought news of him last year—I heard it at Fuggesbroke. He was in good heart and near the end of his studies."

"Then depend on it you'll see him soon."

"I shall be glad—more glad than I can tell."

Her face lit up with a smile which was different from her usual boyish grin. Harman watched her pityingly: Poor lady! she will suffer in her brother's heart as much as in her own. Then he said aloud: "I mun go to my men and see what mischief they're up to on the work. Good night, Mistress Catherine, and keep me in mind."

"Trust me for that, friend. Good night."

Chapter Two

CATHERINE ALARD rode down the hill to Conster Manor. The day had suddenly fallen into twilight, with the coming of a mist over Odimere Ridge, a mist glowing faintly red with the bonfires that still burned along the coast. There was red in the sunset, too, and red on the waters of the River Tillingham, which spread forty feet wide between her and Conster at the foot of the hill. The tide came up as far as the ford, though here it did no more than brim the river; farther down, where the land had not yet been inned, it spread from slope to slope, filling the valley with a great sheet of pearly, mysterious water, flushed here and there with the colours of the sky.

Close to the ford, the Manor drive led from the lane—not very nobly yet, for its oak trees were mere saplings, newly planted by Peter Alard. He had married a rich wife—the Lady Elisabeth Burdett, whose father had been given an earldom and abbey lands in Essex by Thomas Cromwell—and he had long been busy spending her money on Conster and its estates.

He had rebuilt the house almost entirely some twenty years ago. Catherine could dimly remember the old place, with its huge raftered hall, which was always full of the smell of wood-smoke and resin, and its kitchen, nearly as large as the hall and shut off from it only by a wooden screen, so that from her seat at table she could see the fire and watch the little yellow dog that turned the roaster. Masters and servants had all sat down to eat together then, but now these things were changed —to the comfort and relief of the Lady Elisabeth, who for long had bitterly complained of their uncouthness.

The new hall was smaller than the old, and lighter, for Squire Alard, to amuse himself and please his wife, had lanced the walls with windows—which window-taxed Alards of the future would curse and brick up. There was a large, modern fireplace, with handsome dogs and andirons, and the walls were mostly panelled in the modern style, though a few pieces of tapestry hung to jewel the remaining shadows. The kitchen and buttery were now completely shut off, and the daïs in the bay window had become the *privée* parlour, where the family dined and supped.

They were at supper now. Treading through the unlit hall, Catherine could hear their voices in the *privée*. Besides the voices of her parents she could distinguish that of her cousin Kit Oxenbrigge, for the last two years steward of the Alard household, and a fourth voice which had a foreign note in it. She remembered with a grimace that Robert Douce would be there, planning furnaces and bellows and hammerponds for Conster. The grimace was only half smiled off her lips as she entered the room.

"Kate!" cried her mother. "Where have you been? You look like a gipsy."

"Kate!" cried her father in a different voice. "Roiling, roaming, romping Kate! Come, kiss me—'at's a good pug."

Catherine kissed him, and held out her cheek for Robert Douce to kiss—a countrified fashion that made her mother sigh reprovingly.

Elisabeth Alard found it easier to remember that she had been bred up in the French style than that her grandfather had kept hogs in Suffolk. She was a beautiful, graceful woman, dressed harmoniously in dark colours, with pearls braided in her hair. She had been no more than eighteen when her twins were born, and might now be taken for Catherine's sister; for whereas the daughter's skin was already weather-beaten with exposure to sun and wind, the mother's was white and soft as milk and cucumbers could make it.

In looks Catherine was like her father; he too had a dark skin, a wide mouth and prominent eyes, though his eyes were not brown, but a pale, bright Saxon blue—Alard eyes. Kit Oxenbrigge had them, though in other ways he favoured his father's side of the family, with his clean-cut hawk-like profile, from which a dark sweep of hair lay back like a raven's wing. He was not so countrified as his uncle or his cousin, for he had been to Winchester College, and had travelled in France and Italy. His face was shaven, and his speech, though it burred a little, was free of country idiom. Elisabeth Alard spoke the Queen's English in a slow, plaintive voice; Catherine and her father spoke unashamedly the language of the Sussex countryside, with its broad vowels and slurring consonants.

"Where hast thou been, Kate?—the fields an't safe for a maid after dark."

"I went up to Staple to see if the bonfire burned . . . and on my way home I stopped at Holly Crouch. But, Father, a tur'ble thing hath happened—a tur'ble, larmentable thing. They've broken down the cross at Holly Horns."

"By Cock! Who's broken it down?"

"I dunno. Soldiers, I reckon. They say there's been a troop of 'em riding around. When I came there this evening the cross was gone—thrown down and broke in pieces."

"Shame on the deed! But reckon it had to go. I marvel it was let stand so long."

"There's like to be a fresh outbreak against Catholics after this Spanish business," said Oxenbrigge. "Catherine, you must go to church next Sunday."

"I'd sooner die."

"You're a fool!" rapped her mother. "Many parents would have you whipped every time you didn't go, instead of paying your fine."

"Paying's less trouble than whipping. My father's rich."

"I've better things to do with my money than pay for thy non-conformity."

"You might have had to pay for your own."

The Squire's good-natured face darkened.

"None o' that, now, wench! By Cock! there's things I won't endure."

"Eat your supper, Kate," said her mother. "We've all but finished ours."

Catherine sullenly fell to her supper. She loved her father—and her mother too, though a little less. But there was always this question of religion between them—ever since her father had decided to conform. He had kept to the old faith for the first twenty years of the Queen's reign, and his practice had not been attended by those martyrdoms which had visited some of his neighbours. His alliance with a powerful Protestant family—made while that family was suffering eclipse under Queen Mary—had protected him from the full severity of the law, which, moreover, worked less rigorously in the Sussex forests than in more civilized regions. He had maintained his position at the expense of an occasional fine and much private joking with Master Nicholas Pecksall, Vicar of Leasan, who, a priest in Marian orders, said his Mass regularly every Sunday, before opening the church for Morning Prayer.

But everything had been changed by the Papal Bull excommunicating the Queen and the acts of retaliation that followed it. Mass was no longer said in Leasan Church, even behind locked doors, and the Catholic religion, which till then had been no worse than an expensive luxury, had now become High Treason—not only his purse was threatened, but his land and his life. The Burdetts could no longer protect him. It was too much for his easy allegiance, and he conformed, as his wife had long been praying him to do.

Only his children reproached him. He had expected them to conform with him, and it had been a shock to find them so set in the ways he had abandoned. But he was a kindly, easy soul, and after a few efforts at coercion, time wasted in beatings, starvings and tears, he had left them alone. After all, they were nearly of age, and he could not be held responsible for their recusancy. But it had been hard, bitterly hard, for him, when Simon, his only son and Alard's heir, slipped out of the country to be trained for a priest in Rome, thereby forfeiting for ever his inheritance of English land, even life itself should he return.

In comparison, Kate, poor maid, had been no trouble at all. No one could regard the recusancy of a spinster female so seriously as the same offence in a male or even in a married woman. Here again his great Protestant relations had been able to help him, and he knew that as long as he kept his daughter in bounds he had not much to fear. His chief trouble was that no man would marry her—and next to that, that she would talk theology.

She was talking it at this moment to Robert Douce, talking it with her mouth full of pottage, breaking into the tale he loved to tell whenever there was any complaint of harshness against Romanists—of how he had fled from Paris the day after the massacre, with a white kerchief tied round his arm and on that same arm a basket containing the infant Maria disguised with lettuces . . . Catherine had heard that story many times before and always capped it with tales of landless Papists fleeing to Italy and France. When he went on to tell of the kennels of Paris running with Huguenot blood, she would be sure to have a massacre of Catholics to match it with . . . But they were far too much the children of their time to be content with mere controversial anecdotes; from the concrete they passed on to the abstract, from history to theology—now they would be at it for hours . . . and Squire Alard hated theology —he wished it were not so much the fashion. He was relieved when a growing sound in the hall swelled suddenly into a racket.

2

"Lord save us! what is that?" cried Elisabeth Alard. "Husband, we have the noisiest set of servants in the country."

"I'll go and see what's toward," said Kit Oxenbrigge.

"Yes, go—and send them back into the kitchen, I've given

orders many times that only the footmen are to come into the hall."

Oxenbrigge went out, and came back grinning.

"They're asking you to come out, Squire. They say there's an anabaptist in the kitchen, who will tell our fortunes."

"An anabaptist!" cried Elisabeth. "Abominable!"

"'Tis agäunst the law," said her husband. "By Mary-gipsy! I wonder he dare come into a magistrate's house. Bring him here, Kit, and I'll sentence him to the stocks."

"Aye, do," said Catherine. "Most like he's a Gospeller or a Mumpsimus man."

"I never heard of an anabaptist who told fortunes," said Robert Douce in his slow, foreign-sounding English.

Oxenbrigge went out again, and soon came back with a seedy-looking fellow, dressed in the style of a small shopkeeper, in dark homespun and a noggen shirt. In one hand he clutched his shapeless felt hat, in the other a sugar-loaf of stout parchment, black, and pasted with silver stars. Behind him the door was full of the craning, goggling faces of Conster's maids and men.

"A mistake," said Oxenbrigge; "he's no anabaptist, but an astrologer."

"I swear I'm as good a Protestant as anyone here!" cried the stranger. "I came only to see Bess Hallaker, a maid in your ma'ship's and la'ship's service, and to give my blessing on her handfast to your ma'ship's and la'ship's John Fuller—seeing that I'm her uncle, and her father is dead, and her mother, my sister, on the straw with her eighth child. I keep a tallow-chandler's shop in Hastings, but the shops are shut to-day while the bells ring for the glorious victory. So I bethought me to walk into the country, to visit my niece, and brought my philosopher's hat with me to tell her fortune. For years now I've read the future by the stars and by coats of arms. I swear I meant no evil."

"There an't no evil, surelye—save that by telling the future by coats of arms thou breakest the law as surely as if thou refuse baptism. I can send thee to assizes for this."

"My lord! my lord!" cried the poor man, falling on his knees.

Oxenbrigge and Elisabeth Alard laughed loudly, but Catherine was sorry for him, now that she knew he was not one of those terrible Mumpsimus men, who go about mocking the Mass with tin cups and pellets of bone.

"Donna' be scared," she said. "The Squire wöan't hurt 'ee. Put on thy philosopher's hat and read our quarterings. Then thou shalt have a drink of huffcap."

"That's right. Give orders for the law to be broken in my house. Kate's the Squire!"

" 'Tis only a game, Father. The poor old fellow came to make the servants laugh, and now seemingly we've scared him out of his wits."

"That's true, my lord. 'Tis only a game, and one I've played before all the nobility and gentry in these parts. I read the future for Squire Wildigos at Iridge place, and told him on an heir, who came, sure enough, two months later."

"And how big was his lady at the time?" cried Catherine. "Stick to the game, fellow, I counsel thee, or my father will have thee in the stocks."

"Surelye, my lady, surelye. I'm well known here-abouts for an honest man, and for telling honest fortunes. For the gentry I use coats of arms, for the poor folk the stars. I've already told my niece that since her moon is in gemini she may expect to be brought to bed of twins at her second lying-in."

A loud squeal from Bess Hallaker behind the door.

"It would divert me to have our bearings read," said Elisabeth. "We all know it is forbidden only because some fool once foretold the Queen's sudden death."

"Talk not so much of its being forbidden," said her husband, "or I won't have it done here."

In his heart he was a little afraid of the astrologer, afraid yet enticed. He had often wished to have his future read, and would no doubt long ago have sent for some magician, but for his fears, which in reality dissuaded him more than the thought of breaking a law that was often broken.

"By Cock! 'Tis but a game," he said, reassuring himself.

"We'll have it done to tickle the servants," said Elisabeth Alard, moving towards the hall.

She too was a little afraid. Suppose the magician read in her heart the thoughts that grew there for Kit Oxenbrigge . . . She watched Kit as he carried a torch to the fireplace, above which was handsomely carved and painted the Alard coat of arms—a shield argent, three bars gules, on a canton azure a

24

leopard's head or. He held the torch high, to illuminate the carving; the red light shone in his eyes, and she saw fear there —fear like her own.

Then she heard a laugh—careless and heavy. That girl laughed like a ploughboy, and she alone, of all the company, was not afraid.

Ho! Ho! Ho!

"This is he, I understand,
Who killed the blue spider in Blanchpowder Land."

Ho! Ho! Ho!

Catherine laughed again when the magician's cap was on. He looked more seedy and comical than ever with the great black sugar-loaf upon his head. He did not mind her laughing, because she had spoken kindly and had taken his part. He would tell her a fine fortune. He would tell them all a fine fortune, for the matter of that. He knew his business too well to go croaking of sorrow and sickness and death.

"My lords, ladies, gentlemen and good folk all. Harken to the Magus, pupil of that illustrious doctor Polimackeroe-placidus of Switzerland, Doctor of Philosophy, Astrology, Alchemy and Virtue——"

"Who's that, fellow?" interrupted the Squire. "The doctor or thyself?"

"Nobody, Master. 'Tis only a piece I say to begin——"

"Leave it out. Reckon we'll have had enough lies without it."

The old man stammered and fumbled. His piece of rote-learning gave him confidence, helped him to start. Now he hardly knew how to go on, but saved himself by remembering and repeating the last words: "Philida, phileridos, pamphilida, florida, flortos, rub-a-dub."

Then he took out of his belt a little wand, and pointed to the coat of arms upon the wall.

"Of all the noble and ancient families in the land there is none more noble or more ancient than the noble and ancient house of Alard. De Icklesham and de Etchingham were both proud families, but now they are under the crumbling stones. This silver shield stands for eternity, and these stars are Alard's shining sons that shall shine upon the world. That's when I speak for eternity, but when I speak for to-day I see

25

great merrymaking—I see great fires and holly and chop-cherry and blindman's buff, and men and maids dancing round the Lord of Misrule. Ale and pies. There's plenty in Alard's kitchen, and none goes hungry—ale and pies for all. There's a maid's wedding too, and dancing for it and more ale—barrels of ale—and blessings on the bridal bed, and all according to religion. That's for the kitchen. Now let me speak for the hall. There's a wedding in the hall, a grand and noble wedding to a noble lord. That canton azure is blue blood—the bluest blood in the kingdom is proud to mate with Alard's noble lady. She leaves this noble hall to live in a noble castle and to be the mother of seven sons and seven daughters. A golden leopard's head. Simon Alard goes to the Crusades, and rides against the true religion. His sister rides to meet him, and they meet under the cross . . ."

He blinked and stammered as if he were losing the thread of his speech, then he seemed to recover himself, and went on again.

"Aye, indeed, there's a fine marriage for the daughter of the house—noble quarterings, bags of gold and a bridegroom with hair as black as pitch and ebony. I see noble alliances, and great fruitfulness and riches and religion. And for the noble Squire and his lady I too see much wealth. It comes from Alard's land—forests and fields and farms and hamlets, paying tithes and rents and fees. But the riches come from the depth rather than the breadth. I see the fires of many forges, and I hear great bouncing rumblelow, hammers making cannons and cannon-balls. Wars bring riches to Alard, and wheresumever I look I see health and wealth and merrymaking and love-making and religion and long life for all."

He stopped, breathless.

"Well done, fellow!" shouted the Squire. "Thou couldst not have done it handsomer. Thou'st left out nobody and nothing."

"What was it thou wouldst say about my brother Simon?" asked Catherine. "I couldn't understand."

"Mistress, I spoke only of those present."

"Nay, thou didst speak of Simon, going to the Crusades, against the true religion . . . I never heard such rim-ram-ruffe."

"Mistress, I've no memory of it. I never speak of the absent."

He had decided to leave out Simon, not knowing how he was thought of by those at home.

"But thou didst speak of him."

He shook his head, looking bewildered.

"He spoke nonsense," said Elisabeth, who had been pleased to hear of Catherine's marriage, but had rather her bridegroom's hair had not been black.

"Arrant nonsense," said the Squire, "but he shall have a shilling and a glass of huffcap."

"Thank you, my lord, and I can tell you that in all my mortal days as a philosopher I've never seen so fair a fortune as I've seen to-night."

"Ho! philosopher, art thou, maple-face? I thought this was but a game."

The old man remembered his danger, and quickly shed the small air of dignity he had assumed in the heat of what he held to be a good success.

"Surelye, 'tis only a game, my lord—a game to delight the nobility and gentry."

"'At that's right. Now be off. By Cock! thou'rt a valiant mountebank and hast tickled us famously."

The little astrologer bowed, and bowed again, and withdrew amidst much laughter. Everyone was light-hearted because of the good fortune he had told.

3

The servants went shouting and chattering back to the kitchens, full of the thought of Bess's wedding and the good cheer it would bring, though Bess herself did nothing but screech "twins in gemini! twins in gemini!" and run from the hugs and caresses of her sweetheart. The gentry returned to the *privée*, where the Squire poured out some wine.

"Here's to our success. He blessed our plans, Robert Douce —he foretold all that you've been telling me."

"And you believed him? That's wonderful. Foretelling is better than telling, then?"

The Squire looked uneasy.

"Surelye, I an't a child, and I don't believe what I'm told

27

by mountebanks. But it was a valiant good fortune all the same."

"It wants no mountebank to tell there's iron at Conster. Earth and water both declare it, and, besides, it is a matter that hath been known for years."

"By Mack, it hath! But it döan't follow that if we blow a furnace we'll make our fortunes."

"You have many hundreds of acres of forest land to give you timber for the fires."

"Aye, and the fellow said I'd have more."

"Believe him, then, since you find it easier to believe him than to believe me. He knows nothing of iron or of your land, and I smelted iron in Beauface before I became clerk of the works to Sir Philip Sidney. Besides, I have this very day examined every ditch and stream and mount about Conster for the iron that is well known to be there. But believe him rather than me."

"By Mary-gipsy! I tell 'ee I döan't believe him—he's a mountebank, and should be in the stocks. But I'm uncommon glad he told us such a fine fortune. What did 'ee think of thy share of it, Kate?"

"I thought more of what he said about my brother."

"He said näum that was sensible."

"Reckon he didn't, but I should like to understand it for all that."

"There's no understanding it. He only prated—I reckon he started to say summat, and then got scared of what we'd think, and turned it into nonsense."

"He said that Simon would ride against the true religion."

"He'd never do that, surelye, seeing all he's working for it now."

"Husband, you forget!" cried Elisabeth. "The true religion is the Protestant religion."

"Aye, and so it is—I had disremembered. Poor Simon 'ull ride against that, right and sure enough."

"And I ride to meet him?—maybe, that's also true. But I döan't follow what he said about the Crusades and the Cross."

"Maybe it was another Simon he spoke of. 'Tis a name that Alards have been called before this."

"Did a Simon Alard ever go to the Crusades?"

"For shame, thou ignorant girl! Why, Kit here hath his coat

28

of arms from Simon Alard who went to the Crusades and came back with a border of scallop shells for his shield, same as the Oxenbrigges have now. His daughter married an Oxenbrigge and the family took over the Alard arms, seeing that was the end of 'em. Simon Alard had no son."

"Our Simon will have no son."

"No need to tell me that. By Cock! I think enough of it, knowing that all I do will be done for thy cousin Tom—my house with its new porch and hall, my new ploughed lands, my innings on the marsh; aye, and if I blow a furnace it will blow for Tom and his sons and not for Simon and my grandsons. 'Tis hard, hard fortune, and my only comfort's that I'm a lusty man and will most like live eighty years like my father before me."

"If your mountebank spoke truly," said Robert Douce in his softly mocking voice, "you will still have many grandchildren. Did he not promise seven grandsons and seven granddaughters?"

"Aye—out of Kate. She'll have to mend her ways if she looks to get married."

"'A done, do, Father—'a done with baiting me."

"Thou'st not told us yet what thou thinkest of thy fortune."

"And I'll never tell you. I'm going to bed. I'm tired."

"You run about the country all day," said her mother. "No wonder you're tired. Can't you sit for an hour like a gentlewoman? There's your lute. Will you not play it?"

Catherine shook her head.

"No, I'm tired, and I've no heart for music. Good night, Father and Mother. Good night, Master Douce. Good night, Kit."

She bobbed half a curtsy at the room and went out.

"Why is she so sad and heavy all of a sudden?" asked Lady Elisabeth.

"She's thinking of Simon. Poor girl! she loves him dearly."

"It is always sad for twins to be parted," said Robert Douce; "they partake of the same element, and need each other's breath to sweeten the air. I know what I am speaking of, for I left my twin brother in Beauface, and to this day I know not if he's alive or dead."

"Did he follow the Huguenots?" asked Lady Elisabeth.

"He did."

"It is not only the Papists who suffer for their religion, as I often tell Kate."

"No, every man that hath his religion at heart must suffer now. It is the way of the world. A time may come when we shall no longer harry one another, but it will not be any time of ours."

"And maybe when it comes," said the Squire, "'twill be only because religion hath gone cold and an't worth harrying. Now I'm an easy man, and if I had my way Papists could do as they pleased for worship, as long as they said nothing against the Queen. I tell Kate that the day she says a word against the Queen I send her to assizes. But she won't ever say it, for she's a good, loyal maid and hates treason. Now what I would tell you is that I'd have all men worship as they please, so long as 'tis without treason. But is this because I'm a good religious man, who loves my neighbour too much to see him hurt? No, 'tis because one religion seems to me pretty much as good as another and not worth fighting about. Give me my house, my land, my hunting and my hawking and, by Mary-gipsy! I'm a happy man and 'ud let other men alone."

"Is this how we're to spend the evening?" asked Lady Elisabeth, who did not like to see her husband make an exhibition of himself. "I think we have all talked enough. Is there to be no music?"

"I will play for you," said Oxenbrigge.

"Aye, Kit. Take your lute and play to her ladyship while I lay out the land with Mounseer Douce."

The servants had cleared the table of plates and food, and Squire Alard could spread his great map of Conster in the light of the four tall candles that had shone upon their meal. Oxenbrigge wanted no light for his singing and playing. He picked up his lute from the window-seat and came over and sat by Lady Elisabeth in the shadows beside her idle spinning-wheel.

4

"What shall I play?"

"Play me a lavolta."

His long, strong fingers shook the strings into a lively dance. In the shelter of it they could talk.

"Well," she said, "and are you pleased with your bride?"

"Which bride?"

"The conjurer gave you Kate in marriage."

"Indeed! I thought he said her bridegroom was to be rich."

"He will be, when hath married Kate."

"Ah, but I plainly understood that he was to be rich first, in his own right. The prophet spoke of two rich and ancient families."

"The Oxenbrigges are not poor."

"They are beggars beside Alard."

"So, here is a chance of their becoming rich."

He lifted his head, and looked at her full with his piercing, Alard eyes. "Why do you plague me? I've told you many times that I will not marry Kate."

The merry, kicking lilt of the lavolta was ended, and the words "marry Kate" hung on the air. The Squire heard them.

"Aye, that's right. Marry Kate. So, you're trying to persuade him to fulfill his fortune."

"He will not be persuaded."

"It is an honour I've declined before."

"'At that you have! No man will marry poor Kate. Mounseer Douce, I have a daughter whom no man will marry, though a hundred bags o' trash go with her. She can't have Conster, for 'tis entailed on heirs male, but none of my money is tied up with the land. She can have it all."

"She will surely marry soon."

"I wish I thought it. But we've tried a dunnamany matches for her and all have failed. Why won't you have her, Kit?"

Kit laughed, and began another tune.

"Why won't you have her?" whispered Lady Elisabeth.

"You know why I will not."

"She's not so wild but that her husband could tame her; it is having gone husbandless so long that hath made her a wildcat. And as for her religion, tell me not, Kit, that if you had a wife you couldn't make her a Protestant in a night's love."

The unexpected end of the tune again left her words hanging defenceless in silence.

". . . a night's love."

". . . Bloomery cinder."

Robert Douce's words came at the same time and covered them, and for once she felt grateful to that dark, mocking man. She had bitten down on her lip in her first fright . . .

then she wondered why she had been afraid. She was speaking only of Kate.

Oxenbrigge plucked slowly a slow, sad air of Tye's.

"Kit," she repeated, teasing him. "You know that if you made Catherine love you, she would do as you pleased."

"I would not make her love me."

"But you are a man of family and substance. You should marry. Why do you not fall in love?"

" 'Tis because I've fallen in love that I cannot marry."

"Kit . . ."

The ribbons of the lute poured over his arm, and her hand crept under them, the fingers digging and kneading into his flesh, while her hand and her whole arm shook and burned as if with fire. For a moment the music wavered, then slipped without pause into a gayer, louder tune, a hay-de-guy that made the strings thrum and shake and woke great rumbling echoes in the belly of the lute.

5

Upstairs in her bedroom Catherine could hear the music. Her room was not directly over the *privée*, but a little to one side of it, though near, looking northward over the River Tillingham to where a steep hillside lay black against the stars. If she leaned out of the window she could see the spread waters of the eastern valley, the tidal lake that stretched between Pesenmarsh and Odinmere. But to-night she did not lean out, choosing to sit at her window and watch the stars.

She had sent away Nan Jordan, her woman, because she wanted to be alone, and also because she had never liked the process of being dressed and undressed. She could dress and undress herself and arrange her own hair—not to her mother's satisfaction but to her own. To-night she loosened her bodice and let it fall from her shoulders. The window was unglazed, and she enjoyed the heresy of the night air. Many and many a time they had told her she would die early, but here she was, still alive, though unwed.

A dreamy smile changed and softened her face. Unwed . . . wed . . . the unwed may be wed . . . She knew it was folly to believe the words of conjurers, and against religion too, but there was pleasure in a good fortune all the same. Her bridegroom's hair was to be black as pitch and ebony. . . . She had often wanted to put her hand on Kit Oxenbrigge's head, and push and flatten that shining lock of hair. Black as pitch . . . pitch black . . . black Protestant . . . but she could change him—his Protestant roots could not be deep. The green bay tree has only just been planted in the land and can easily be plucked up . . .

But he would not have her. The rub was there rather than in religion. He had been asked to have her, and would not. She knew that and had been told. No one would have her, because she was a Papist, and too masterful for most—and now she was growing past the age . . . and it is against religion to believe the words of conjurers.

Sighing deeply, she put her elbows on the sill, and cupping her chin in her hands, stared up at the glittering sky. Then the music began. She knew that Kit's fingers were plucking it for her, plucking it and sending it up to her without knowing or caring if she heard it. Down in the parlour it was a merry tune, but as the notes crept out the night breathed on them and turned them to sadness. It was a sad melody that reached her ears, making her feel sad, with a sadness that was part of the night, of the black, sighing trees, and the tunnels under the trees, and the wild, shaggy places of the garden, the ghostly waters of the river, and the far-off dazzle of the stars.

She knew that the stars were set in spheres, crystal spheres girdling the earth, and that these spheres made music, singing together a song so sweet and loud that it is silence. Her mind made play that this music creeping to her from the darkness was the music of the spheres, tinkling and singing eternally, the music of the stars in their solemn, far-off houses. But every now and then her heart would remember Kit Oxenbrigge's hands upon the lute, and his sleek head bent towards it; she would think of putting out her hand to stroke that head. . . . Such thoughts had nothing to do with the music of the spheres, and soon her mind fell back to earth.

Why must she have a different lot from the lot of the women round her, who married and bore children? In spite of her wildness, of her boyish looks and ways, she wanted to be married. Not only was she the child of a day which knew the spinster only as a monstrosity—an unreckoned and sinister fruit of the Dissolution—but she wanted love and the fulfilment of her body in childbearing. Already, at twenty-eight and hale as a lad, she seemed to feel the life in her wither as she watched girls ten years younger than herself suckle and lead their children. Once or twice she had been asked in marriage by men she barely knew, but that had been years ago, before her need was great. Then she had refused to take a Protestant, and now it seemed that no Protestant would take her. Of late years no one had even approached her, in spite of the money that would go with her; she knew that Oxenbrigge had been her parents' last hope. . . .

"Oh, God," she prayed, "stop the music!"

It did not stop just then, but a little later. The night was suddenly healed with silence. Her heart found balm in the smell of the dew; leaning out of the window she could smell the dew, and it was comforting as the smell of a friend. The night was black round Conster, with the tall, shadowing trees and the waters ebbed from the valley. Only when she lifted her eyes could she see the stars above the hill—Starvencrow Hill, it was called, and she knew the lines of it as well as the lines of her own body. She watched the lines of the hill and of the strip of firmament above, the firmament of the northern constellations, where the Plough heels slowly round the pole-star, and Cassiopœia sits glimmering in her chair, and Pegasus lights the corners of a black field.

Many times she and Simon had watched the stars from this window, telling their names and counting them in their bunches. When she thought of Simon she could pray. . . . It was no longer just a prayer of relief, for the music to stop, but the prayer of her own voice talking to God: "Oh, God, Thou hast become my firmament and my refuge, and in Thee will I put my trust. . . . Oh God, my firmament. . . ."

After all, if she was to be a stranger in her own land, she was only sharing her brother's fate. Simon must always be a hunted stranger, so why should she seek a country? She and Simon were the lost boy and girl of the Alards—lost in the wood of a strange faith but with the unchanging firmament above them, the immovable starry sky, pricked with the lights of heaven. She need not fear when she was with Simon; she wanted no black Protestant to pluck her out of the wood and shut her from the stars. Better far be lost with Simon where she could see those set and faithful stars; and perhaps one day she would really hear their music, instead of being earthbound with the music of a lute.

What was it the old mountebank had said? "Simon Alard rides to the Crusades, against the true religion—and his sister rides to meet him." That was strange, though doubtless she would ride to meet him if she knew when he would come.

"They meet under the cross"—that certainly was not true, for the cross was broken down. Heigho! there are no crosses in the land—they are all broken down. The conjurer must have been wandering in his wits . . . and anyway 'tis all superstition.

Chapter Three

WHEN SHE woke next morning, the sun was bright on Starvencrow Hill, lighting its crown of wild gold, and above it, instead of the stars, blazed the blue summer north, swept by the wind that still tore after King Philip's navy. Catherine found, as she had found so often, but always with sweet surprise, that sorrow had passed with the night.

She jumped out of bed and dressed herself in the old clothes she loved and her mother despised. Her mother was ashamed of her because she did not wear stays or ruff or farthingale, but clothes such as the country ladies wore before the new fashions came in—a bodice and partlet and full, short skirt, ample to stride a horse in.

Her mother was still in bed, and when she rose would be dressing for an hour. But her father was up and had already gone out to his dogs and his hawks. Catherine did not wish to meet him, for she was just about to start for Fuggesbroke, and she knew that he would not approve of her going there. Her position as the nonconforming daughter of a magistrate was already delicate enough without her openly visiting recusants.

Yet Agnes Tuktone, though younger than herself and bred to stop at home, had been her friend for many years—ever since Simon had gone to Rome, before which day she had not needed friends. Now she needed them, and there was only Agnes Tuktone and Nicholas Pecksall—whom she scarcely al-

lowed herself to count as a friend, seeing that he was a runagate priest who had abjured his religion, but whom she must
still go and see because he had been Simon's tutor and she
could talk about him. She must see Agnes too, and every now
and then she slipped away to Fuggesbroke, since Squire Tuktone kept his daughters close at home and would not let them
ride about the country like some others. To-day it was important that she should go, because she wanted to tell Agnes and
her parents about Thomas Harman and hear maybe how soon
there would be a chance of a priest to reconcile him.

She made her way to the stables, and was lucky to avoid
being seen by her father while she waited for her horse. In a
few minutes she was in the saddle and away up the hill, thudding in a gay, short canter over the turf and heather, then
through the gorse to the edge of Holly Crouch's fields—corn
and pasture, hedged and tilled among all the wild acres of
commonland.

She avoided the house, and skirting the western rim of
Dodyland Shaw, came to the Horns. Her face darkened as she
looked at the empty air which till yesterday had been signed
with a cross. It grew darker when she saw some men at work
among the fallen stones, looking as if they meant to cart them
away.

"Where are you taking those?"

"To Master Harman—to build his new house."

"To build his house!—but 'tis sacrilege. They're holy
stones."

"He told us to bring 'um."

Catherine said no more. The stones belonged to Thomas
Harman . . . But she had a mind to say nothing for him at
Fuggesbroke. For the moment he seemed to her only a little
better than the impious men who had thrown down the cross
. . . But the next her heart relented. She had known him too
long to run against him, and she could not bear to think of
him dying in the cold and darkness outside the true religion.
Maybe he had taken these stones out of fear—hoping that with
them some of the old protections might be built into his new
house. She must not grudge him the comfort of a few stones.

Turning her horse's head, she came out on the road by
Haneholt's Wood, and followed the westward way as far as
the farmstead known as Colespore. Here she dipped into a

rutted track that led from the farm to its Manor of Fuggesbroke, down in the valley by the Pipingclay stream. Fuggesbroke was an old grim house, of Caen stone, built round with many walls and barns. It had a shut, withdrawn look, and seemed to frown upon the stranger. Nobody was about—there was no laughing and quarrelling of men and maids among the barns; indeed, the place seemed deserted—and yet it watched.

Catherine rode up to the shut door and rattled the bars. An old man suddenly appeared—pottering in the yard, which was empty of beasts.

"Ned," cried Catherine. "Is your mistress up?"

He glared at her suspiciously.

"Pox on you, Ned! you know me—Mistress Catherine Alard of Conster Manor, come to see Mistress Tuktone."

Mumbling and mouthing at her, he opened the gate and she rode in, her horse's hoofs clattering strangely in the empty place. He left her while he went into the house, and in a few moments a girl came out—Agnes Tuktone.

"Kate! dearest Kate! Forgive such a paltry greeting; but old Ned can think of nothing but soldiers after last year."

"Even when 'tis a woman riding alone? He hath some valiant notions." She slid from her saddle, and they kissed.

"Come in, dear Kate, and see my mother. She's in the winter parlour with Susanna and Margaret."

They went in together. The house was old and dark and grim. It had none of Conster's elegancies and modernities; the windows were few and only partly glazed, and in the great hall a strew of rushes still made the only carpet. The walls were naked stone and the hangings spare, for a year ago the house had been raided by a priest-hunting band of soldiers, and nearly everything of value had been carried off. At the end of the great hall, by the kitchens, was the bare little parlour where Mistress Tuktone sat spinning with her two young daughters.

She might have been any age between forty and sixty, for she was erect and thin as a girl, and yet her face was a lined map of many years. The skin had the clearness of youth, but also a yellowish pallor which was the parchment of age rather than the milk of youth. The eyes were black as coals, and like coals blazed in a fire, which might have been youth's ardour or age's consuming bitterness. When she saw Catherine she smiled, and her smile placed her definitely among the old, for it was bitter.

"Welcome, Kate. You're timely this morning."

"So timely," said Agnes, "that she could scarce get in. Old Ned would have shut the gate on her."

"You mustn't blame him. In our present state 'tis better that he should keep good folk out than let bad folk in."

"You think this house is like to be searched again?" asked Catherine.

"What else can I think, now this new trouble's come upon us with the Spanish navy? Likewise, they found nothing last time, so I reckon they'll go on searching till they find."

"They'll never find. Since all your gear is stowed in the hide, it will never be found."

"Wretched girl! So you would tempt heaven with your craking! Some day, by the malice of Satan, our hide will be found. When last the soldiers were here they did naught but march about, rapping the walls and stamping the floors. I gave us up for lost a dozen times."

"But each time our Guardian Angel saved us," cried Susanna. "I reckon he's a match for any malice of Satan. Mother, you must have faith."

"Aye—that is what your father says."

She sighed, and looked round upon her children.

"When will there be Mass here again?" asked Catherine.

"Hush! We know not. Never, maybe."

"Oh say not so! 'Tis more'n a twelvemonth since a priest came. One is sure to come soon."

"Do not talk of it."

"But I mun talk of it; for Master Thomas Harman of Holly Crouch Yard asked me yesterday if he may come here when Mass is said again."

"Thomas Harman! But he conforms."

"He hath conformed till now; but now he's growing old and sick, and like many around here his heart hath been always with the old religion."

"Then why did he follow another?"

"Only to spare his pocket. He never believed in the new book—the proof is that now he's asking for the old one."

"That proves nothing. He may be coming as a spy to sell us all."

"He'd never sell us!" cried Catherine indignantly; "he's an honest man."

"He's a conformer—a traitor. He's sold his children's birthright for a few pieces of gold. How can I believe that he wouldn't sell us too?"

"You know, Mother," pleaded Agnes, "that our Church is merciful to those poor folk who go to the Protestant service out of their poverty."

"Harman can't plead poverty. He can pay for his religion as well as any, and better than some."

"He told me," said Catherine, "that he conformed because until lately he was careless of religion. But now he hath a sickness which he thinks is unto death—and he's scared to die out of the Church."

"Mother!" cried Margaret. "We daren't deny him."

"Think, child. You've forgotten that his son is to marry Maria Douce, whose father is a Protestant spy."

"Mounseer Douce an't no spy," said Catherine, speaking more surely than she felt.

"My child, no doubt they all are honest men. The young are quick to trust, not having learned harder wisdom. One day you will know that even an honest man will tell a secret to save his skin. Was it not our own John Gaine, who had served us from boyhood and whom we had treated as a son, who betrayed us this last time? And now I hear Father Oven is taken and will be brought to trial at Chichester. His blood be on that wicked man's head."

"Is Father Oven taken?" cried Catherine.

"Yes, we heard last week that he was taken at Battle. They are all taken, our priests, one by one. Soon we shall be sheep without a shepherd—the wolves will have gotten them all."

2

As her voice sank on its bitter note, footsteps sounded on the stone floor outside; the next moment the door opened and Squire Richard Tuktone came in. All the women rose.

"Why, Kate! This is a pleasure."

He kissed her.

He was like his wife in height and complexion, but on his face youth did not strive with age, seeming rather to have made some fortunate treaty with it. His hair was nearly white, and his face was worn, but lit up from within, as if the yellow-ish skin stretched upon the bones were the fine horn of a lant-horn. His hands were spoiled with work, for the Tuktones were too poor to pay ploughmen and field labourers, and the Squire and his sons worked in their own fields. By the same token, his dress was scarcely more than a labouring man's, but he wore it with neatness and dignity.

"Kate hath a plot," said his wife; "a plot that will hang us all."

"That sounds a valiant plot. Tell us more of it, Kate."

" 'Tis for reconciling Thomas Harman of Holly Crouch Yard."

"That good old man! I've often thought it sad that such as he should favour heresy."

"He doth not favour it in his heart. His heart always hath been with us, and now he would follow his heart, and hath asked that he may be told when next there's a priest at Fuggesbroke."

"*Deo gratias*," said Richard Tuktone.

"Nay, not *Deo gratias*," said his wife, "but *miserere nobis*. It will be our ruin if Thomas Harman comes to Fuggesbroke."

"How so?"

"Already our secrets are known to too many."

"They are known to a bare half-dozen outside this house."

"But one of those hath already shown us how lightly she sets by our lives."

"For shame, wife! That's no way to talk of Kate. I'm with her in this. If Thomas Harman wishes to be reconciled we imperil our souls if we forbid him."

"Maybe he is a spy and asks only to betray us."

"Thomas Harman a spy? Sweet love, your fears outrun your wits. I'd as soon doubt one of my own sons."

"He may be forced to betray us for his skin. Oh, husband, we should be mad to listen to Kate. We shall all be taken, and this time it won't be only our land and our fortune, but our lives . . . Kate can't understand. Her father is a magis-trate and he protects her; she can't know the sufferings of families like ours which are marked down for persecution. We had far better stay as we are and keep our religion soberly among ourselves. If we add to our number we only add to the number of our betrayers."

40

"My sweet Mary, have I not said that you're too much shaken? Our Lord and Saviour suffered the traitor Judas for three years rather than break the company of the Apostles. Our duty an't only to our household, but to this poor starved country."

"I know, I know," mourned the poor lady, "but it an't for myself I fear. I see my husband and sons being led away . . . Kate can't understand . . . and all because we won't be advised, but take risks which bring good to no one."

"Is there no good," asked Catherine, "in a Protestant being reconciled?"

"I should fear," said Agnes, "if I stood in the way of such a deed."

"Aye, I know well—I know I am a coward. But you must forgive me, Kate, and think how terrible it is for us with these new laws. We're like rats being smoked in a hole—we can't leave, and we're harried all the time we stay. Our beasts and cattle have been taken from us, and our fines have brought us to poverty. And now, after this attack from Spain, we go in fear of our lives. Mark me, all will be worse after this—they will say it is a Catholic plot, that we wanted to have the King of Spain over . . . Oh that the great foreign kings would think of us poor English Catholics and how we suffer for their politics— and the Jesuits, too, who never care if they live or die . . . I wish they'd remember there are Catholic women in England."

"My sweet soul," said the Squire, "you talk as if God gave less grace to women than to men. If He asks you for your life, I warrant that by His grace you'll give it as gladly as you gave your fortune."

"Aye—but what if He asks for yours?"

"If He ever does me that honour, I'll trust Him for you as well as for me. But we an't come to that yet; and you mustn't think I shall act without common prudence. I will see Harman and sound him before I make any promises or tell any secrets. So take heart, gentle Mary, and think of poor Kate, who I know is starved, as indeed we all are at this time of day. Let's go to our breakfast."

3

Catherine breakfasted with the Tuktones—the Squire and his lady, his servants, his daughters, his sons, his sons' wives, one of whom had a child at her breast and the other a child in her womb. It was a plain meal, of oaten bread and ale that was little more than huffcap, eaten off wooden platters, all the pewter and silver having gone in the last loot. But Catherine enjoyed it, for she was hungry as a crane, having left last evening her father's table so suddenly in such disgust that she had neglected to take up her portion for the night.

She was glad to be at Fuggesbroke, in spite of Mary Tuktone's bitterness. She liked the girls, who were merry enough, she even liked the sad, slow-eating sons, who seemed weighed down, as if with care for their wives and their young families. Richard Tuktone she loved, though she saw him rarely. He made this sad business of religion somehow seem gay and glorious, putting into it a new kind of hope, which was independent of politics, so that for once she could forget her cares and her contrivings, and could feel that nothing mattered so long as she served her neighbour and kept her heart in grace.

He was telling them at table of the execution of Father Thomas Pilchard of Battle, which had taken place at Dorchester in the west a year ago, but of which he had only just received the account from a friend.

"Seemingly there was a reason why they couldn't have the town executioner, so some cook or butcher was hired in his place, and proved such a lobber at his work that it was only half done, and Jack Huddleston writes that in the end the priest threw out his own bowels, crying *'miserere mei'*."

The company was not squeamish, but the women shuddered, and Mary Tuktone crossed herself.

"Poor soul!" murmured Alice, the young mother, "and 'tis scarce two years since he sat at this table . . . he baptized our little Richard . . ."

"Ah," sighed Jane Tuktone, "who will baptize my poor baby when it comes?"

"The grandfather," said the Squire, "if no priest can be found. But maybe the sufferings of our martyrs will send us a priest. Our God shall no more forsake Alice and Jane Tuktone than He forsook those holy martyrs Perpetua and Felicitas— your patrons in the court of heaven, since they stood before their persecutors carrying their babes, born and unborn. You are my Perpetua and my Felicitas, and must remember the jest Saint Austin once cracked upon your names, and be of perpetual felicity."

Then he spoke of other things, of farming and his hopes for the land at Fuggesbroke and Colespore, of the cattle they still kept, and of the birds and conies and wildcats in the woods. For next to his faith and his family, he loved his country-side, and to study the ways of wild creatures. He told Catherine that he preferred the wisdom of the fields and woods to the wisdom of books, and the wisdom of the stars to the wisdom of the astrologers. He knew the names and motions of the stars, and followed Saint Austin in holding that their purpose was to proclaim the glory of God rather than to rule the fates of men.

4

As soon as breakfast was over, Catherine set off homewards, well pleased with her morning's work. She had done her best for Thomas Harman, and felt that she could rely on Richard Tuktone to bear down his lady's fears and opposition. She hesitated whether she should call at Holly Crouch and report her doings; then decided that she had better leave the next move to Tuktone—and that if she saw Harman she was at the moment more likely to quarrel with him than console him, on account of those stones . . . She would ride back to Conster.

No, she would not . . . Her eye had caught the tower of Leasan Church rising out of the huddle of Leasan roofs, a mile from the Horns, and she felt moved to ride down the eastward lane and call on Nicholas Pecksall at the Parsonage. It was over a fortnight since she had seen him, and though she did not hold with his ways she found that her life seemed to hang empty about her if many days went by without their meeting.

Their friendship—if such it could be called, for they spent most of their time in argument—sprang out of the relations of master and pupil. She and Simon had had no other tutor than the Vicar of Leasan. From him she had learned Latin and French, history, philosophy, theology, the greater and lesser mathematics, though she could not say that all this had stayed in her head as it had stayed in her brother's. Nor had she ever studied so hard, but had idled and watched the window, and no doubt would have had many a rap from her master's cane if he had not been a soft-hearted, sensitive man, who hated to hurt anything, even a naughty child.

To-day she found him in his garden, which, with his books, was his great delight.

"Welcome, Catherine! I wondered when you would come again to see me. Let me call Alice to fetch you some ale."

"I thank 'ee. But I've breakfasted at Fuggesbroke."

It pleased her to provoke him with the name.

He looked back at her and mumbled something; then he said:

"Tie your horse to the fence and come and sit in my arbour. If you must talk of Fuggesbroke you'd better talk of it off the King's highway."

"I an't a-going to talk of Fuggesbroke, but I'll come and sit in your arbour."

She came in at the gate and they went together to an arbour of roses opening to the north. From it they could see the small, snug parsonage with its thatched roof, and the brown church that sat among the thickets like a hen. Immediately before them lay the garden, the parson's pleasance, stocked with rose trees, gillyflowers, pansies, heliotrope and lavender, all scenting the sunshine. It was a sweet spot, and a kind of angry sadness seized the girl as she looked round on it; she felt that it was for this earthly paradise that Nicholas Pecksall had compromised his heaven.

"Since when is it unsafe to talk of Fuggesbroke?" she exclaimed. "I remember that when last I was here you rated me a full hour for going there."

"I said only that 'tis not safe to talk of it on the highway. Likewise, you forget that since you last came here a Spanish navy sailed from Spain, and that to-day were it not for the weather the Spaniards would be restoring the true religion with swords, bilboes, pikes, arquebuses and ordnance."

"You shouldn't speak so."

"I speak the truth. The people of England are roused up by such an assault. Depend on it, persecution will begin, and what it would have been safe to speak of a month ago it now isn't safe to think of."

"Safe! safe!—that's your most precious word."

"'Tis a golden word. For it means salvation."

"Your safety will never lead to your salvation."

44

"I'm not so sure. But listen, Kate. I'm not careful for my-self alone. I think of others. Without talking high of martyrs as some do, I've no wish to see anyone in prison, least of all you, dear Kate."

"You needn't fear for me. My father's daughter will never be sent to prison."

"I shouldn't count on that, if you consort with Fuggesbroke. Remember that Squire Tuktone is suspected of harbouring priests, setting up the Mass, and having a daughter a nun in Rheims."

"It looks as if Squire Tuktone cared less for safety than for salvation."

"It would be better if he cared more. It would have been better for us all if there had been fewer hot-heads among us. It is such men as Tuktone who have brought us half our troubles. If he and his like had conformed, they might still be hearing Mass in their parish churches. Courage is one of the virtues, but others are prudence, soberness and sense."

"I call 'em vices—the vices of the new clergy."

"And you rank me as one of those?"

He was angry with her now, swinging round at her on the seat. Anger made him look young. Till then, though he was not more than fifty-five, he had seemed an old man, pottering in his garden with his cassock bunched about his middle. But now she saw his eyes kindle with a fire that made them sud-denly the eyes of a young man.

"You rank me as one of those?" he repeated harshly.

"Why not, since you've cast in your lot with them?"

"I have Catholic orders—I'm not one of Cranmer's men."

"But you've never said Mass since the day the Queen of Scots was beheaded—that was the end of your ministry."

He suddenly grew calm—and old again.

"You know well that I said Mass openly in Leasan Church for five years after the Queen came to the throne; and after that, for fifteen years, I said it in secret before I said Morning Prayer on Sundays. I gave it up only when we older parish priests were all convened to Chichester and told that this cus-tom of saying our Mass in secret must end—that our oath of supremacy would not save us so long as we mixed the old religion with the new. That was when I gave up saying Mass. I had no choice."

"You had the choice of leaving your parish. I'll never understand how a priest of the true Church could stay."

"As for that, there's many a priest of the true Church reading Morning Prayer in England at this hour. To go no further, there's old Master Beswyke at Odimere, put there under King Harry and stayed through King Edward and the Common Prayer, and then went back to the missal under Queen Marie and is now back to the Common Prayer again. And Master Eyot who died of the plague at Delmonden was put in by Cardinal Wolsey—and up and down the country you'll find the same. Why should we priests care more than our people, who do not give a rap either for the Mass or for Common Prayer? None cares for religion in this country, though nothing else is talked of."

"You should come out openly," she muttered.

"I'll come out the day my folk come out."

"You know they'll never do that."

"I know. If they'd come out thirty years ago we'd have had none of this trouble now. But they didn't care enough, and they still don't care."

"Maybe they don't care; but they're poor witless sheep, without a shepherd."

"And you ask me to lead them out into the wilderness? I might lead, but they wouldn't follow; and if I went out some gospeller would be put in to preach heresies—at least they learn no heresies from me. There is a virtue in expediency."

"You're learning me a whole new set of virtues."

"Virtues that are needful in such times as these. Remember, Kate, that if I counsel you, I was once your master, and you are still a dear child to me."

His face lit up as he spoke with an enchanting kindness. She felt her anger against him ooze away, but she tried to keep some of it.

"I an't a child, but a grown woman. And I mun go my own way since I care not for yourn."

"But your way leads to nothing, or rather to destruction. I can't stand by and see you destroy yourself for nothing."

"Nothing! Is that how you call our religion? Have you come to that?"

"No, but this country hath. Our religion's nothing to this

country and we must learn to live without it. They have pulled down the great Church and built a little slab castle, but even so we have a roof over our heads. Let us be thankful."

"If I believed you, I should want to die."

She sat beside him with her throat lifted tragically, her eyes alight with tears. He wondered that she should care so much.

"Catherine, there are other things in life."

She looked round on the sunny, flowery garden, on the thatched parsonage, the nestling church, on his housekeeper, suddenly appeared in the door with a summons to dinner.

"There are other things in life," he repeated, and his voice was like the smell of his roses.

"Aye," she said sadly. "I see that there are other things."

"And must you despise them? Can't you enjoy them too? Must you always be seeking and craving for what you never can have? Kate, 'tis your own fault that you're unhappy."

"I an't unhappy," she said, clenching her teeth.

"Poor child," he murmured, "poor child."

"A-done, do, with pitying me."

"I pity you for your plottings. You live in a coil. But there's a straight path in life."

"Not for such as I."

"Believe me, for such as you, if you would set your feet on it."

"'Tis a path that leads to hell."

"No—into a rose garden."

"Your roses eat the air—I cannot breathe," she cried, and stood up to go.

"No, do not go. You're only just come. Stay a while and talk to me of Simon."

"Simon! why should I talk to you of him? His path's more like to lead to a gallows than a rose tree."

"We'll not talk of him as he is now, but as he used to be in the days when you and he came riding together from Conster. I remember a watchet gown you wore. You were a piece of sky on your white horse."

"And Simon rode a brown mare—it broke my heart when my father would sell her after he was gone, for I saw him astride her still."

She stayed another hour, for she loved to talk of Simon,

and this man's kindness would sometimes make amends for his apostasy.

Chapter Four

DURING THE weeks that followed, Catherine went only seldom to Fuggesbroke. She found herself no longer welcome there. Richard Tuktone and Agnes were as kind as ever, but of necessity she saw little of the Squire, and Agnes was restrained by her mother's mood, which daily grew more opposed to Catherine's visits. Because of this scheme of hers for reconciling Thomas Harman, she thought her mad, rash, wild, untrustable, and as well kept out of their sight as out of their counsels.

There was a time when Mary Tuktone would have been as glad as any to welcome back a lost sheep to the fold. But during the last ten or twelve years local opinion had hardened against Romanists in general and Fuggesbroke in particular, and repeated attacks had set up defences of suspicion and fear. An intermittent persecution had culminated a year ago, when Fuggesbroke was "beaten up" by a party of soldiers, searching for plunder which they could not find but the hope of which they would certainly not abandon. Since then Mary Tuktone's heart had seemed to contract and embitter.

She lived in a constant anxiety—for her husband, for her daughters, for her sons, and for her grandchildren. The spoliation of her property she could accept, and the poverty into which they were slowly sinking as Sunday by Sunday brought their distraint for non-conformity—twenty pounds a month for each member of the household who did not attend the parish church. She could bear to see her furniture and hangings sold, to exchange silver for earthenware and pewter for wood, to listen to the echoes of her empty yard, spin stammell yarn and eat black bread; but she could not bear to think of the daily danger in which her husband went with his sons—every trotting horse upon the road put terror in her heart. Nor could she overcome her terror for her daughters, keeping them close like chickens under a hen, fearing that if they strayed they would be ravished by ruffians who knew that the law moves slowly for Papists though swiftly against them.

To this black mood Catherine Alard's impunity was a daily irritation. It seemed to her a grievous thing that she should be protected by her mother's heresy and her father's apostasy, and sometimes, weakened as she was by privation and fear, she would taunt her with it, cutting Catherine's heart.

"But what can I do?" the girl cried angrily. "Should I go calling around the magistrates and asking them to take me?"

"No, but you can remember those who haven't your good luck."

"And when do I forget them?"

"My good girl, every time you speak of their affairs to strangers."

"Mistress Tuktone, that an't true by me. I've never spoken of Fuggesbroke to a soul save Thomas Harman and maybe sometimes to Master Pecksall."

"They are both runagates. Thomas Harman hath been scared into Catholicism by a few pains, and could certainly be scared back into Protestantism by half as many more. As for Nicholas Pecksall, he is a traitor to his priesthood and our holy religion. I think no good of you for entering his house."

Catherine was moved to answer:

"But he is a kind man."

"Judas was kind—and kissed."

Catherine felt too angry to say more, and soon afterwards went home. Sometimes she thought that if a priest came to Fuggesbroke she would hear of it only by the charity of Richard Tuktone—that his wife would do all that she could to keep her away.

It was now full time that a priest should come again, and yet there was no rumour of him. Sometimes she feared that her plight was worse even than Mary Tuktone sought to make it and that no priest would ever come. Two of those who used to visit Fuggesbroke had been taken in the last two years— Father Pilchard was dead and Father Oven lay in Chichester gaol awaiting trial; and though rumours of the daily landing of Jesuits spread through an affrighted country-side—scared by the Armada into its first real Protestantism—Catherine knew them to be mere tales. The mills of Douay, Rheims and Rome ground slowly, and scattered their seed of martyrs thinly on English soil. Meanwhile the Catholics of England went hungry, and, like hungry men, brought up wind.

Cut off in this way from those who should have been her friends, Catherine went more often to Leasan Parsonage. She might argue and wrangle with Pecksall, but there were times when she found a queer kind of peace in sitting with him in his arbour and talking of common, indifferent things. For those days her mind was like a goad, pricking her continually, so that like a goaded horse she was always in a sweat. Her mind pricked her every hour with the bitterness of Mary Tuktone and the slowness of religion, with longing for her brother away in Rome, and with queer, hankering thoughts of another kind, that she smothered and repented of.

Nicholas Pecksall was one of her goads, but there was comfort in the man. He had always been a kind man, and now she felt the attraction of his kindness. Also he would talk to her about her brother, tenderly of him in the past, carefully of him now—he would never offend her on the topic of Simon. If they quarrelled it would be only when the wounds that her mind gave her itched, and it eased her to rub them with an argument.

There was a reason why she went besides that which she gave herself. She felt an urge to escape from Conster, and now that Fuggesbroke frowned on her there was nowhere else for her to go. Conster had changed of late. There was something dark at Conster which perplexed and scared her. She did not know where the shadow lay—it seemed to move about like a ghost. Sometimes she thought it was in Robert Douce's black eyes, staring at her across the table while his mouth talked with her father. Sometimes it would lie in Oxenbrigge's, as shadows lie in the sea. She would see it moving in his eyes as he turned them from her father's face to her mother's— then she would think for a moment that she saw it in her mother's . . . it could be nowhere but in her own heart— black eyes, blue eyes and grey must all be innocent, and only her heart see ghosts in its own darkness.

She argued with her fears. If only she could make them solid they would be fears no longer, only dislikes which she could recognize and frustrate. Of course the reason why Robert Douce made her feel uncomfortable was, she told herself (apart from the fact that he was rumoured as a Huguenot spy), that he encouraged her father in his plans to spoil Conster. He would spoil it entirely to make it rich. Already she had heard many times what he would do.

A furnace was to be built about half a mile down the River Tillingham, on land which had already been inned for a small farm, known as Glaseneye, on the hill above. This farm could be reached from Leasan by a lane known as Ferthinglond, and there was another lane running to it from Conster Manor itself. The place was therefore well served with roads, and had moreover the river to link it with the port of Rye.

Still better was it served with timber. The great forest of Wogenmarye spread from Odimere Ridge to the Kentish border, while to the west lay the forest of Medyresham, not so large, but covering a thousand acres between Redelond and Vinehall. These woods were not all the property of Alard—they had mostly belonged to Battle Abbey before the dissolution and were now the loot of many small Squires—the Broomfields of Odimere, the Goodsells of Bread and the Austens of Redelond. But Alard had money to buy them, either standing or as timber, and they would feed Conster Furnace for more than a hundred years.

Catherine's heart was sad when she thought of those wild, lovely woods, where she and Simon had sought and shared so many adventures, being cut down to feed the fires that were to make vulgar iron gates and railings for the vulgar new nobility that Protestantism had set up. The fact that they would also make cannon and cannon balls for the overthrow of England's enemies was only a slight vindication, when she thought of the railings and the gates and their conceited ornaments, and when she thought of the terrible waste-hills and cinder-heaps that would rise above Conster, where now all was forest and moorland and fruitful field. She once had ridden through Ashburnham and seen the smitten woods, and amidst their ruin those sinister dark hills. She had seen the glare of the furnaces wash out the stars, and had heard the thud and boom of the hammers like giants marching through the night. All this would come to Conster . . . and she worked herself into a frenzy of hate and opposition, telling herself all the while that it was the reason why she shunned Robert Douce.

She found it more difficult to reason away her fear of Oxenbrigge and her fear of her mother. She told herself that her fear of Oxenbrigge was love. It was not a good love, not a love for his soul, but for his fine body and his clever, comely mind. Sometimes while she watched him her heart would ache almost to tears, just to see the black sweep of his hair from his brow, his clear hawk-like face, with the shaven chin above his ruff, and his clothes and air which were so different from the clothes and air of other men she knew—so cleanly, gay and gallant. His mind was gay and gallant too, whether he talked or sang or played the lute. He was a fine gentleman compared with them all at Conster, and sometimes when he played the lute she saw herself dancing in the great hall as his bride.

But she knew that he did not love her and he would never marry her, conjurer or no conjurer. When he tired of his stewardship at Conster he would ride home to his own manor of Oxenbrigge, his father's house by Iden on the Kentish border, and marry some Protestant lady . . . He would do that if he did not something much more dreadful first . . .

Once she had seen a look fly between him and her mother —a dark look on black wings. It had flown from his eyes to her mother's and back again, and now it was one of the shadows of the house. In the shadow she could hear voices murmuring . . . "dear love" . . . "dear heart" . . . She was afraid, terribly afraid, and shocked and ashamed. Sometimes she told herself she was dreaming it all, that her imagination was astray; she had set her course by a flying look—by a bird.

But before that he had sung a song to his lute:

"The beggar Love that knows not where to lodge,
    At last within my heart when I slept,
        He crept,"

and she had seen her mother's hand holding Oxenbrigge's under the ribbons of the lute.

She tried to reason away her fear of her mother. She feared her mother, she told herself, because she loved her and because her mother would never leave her in peace. She was always scolding after Catherine: "Why are you always uncombed and undressed? . . . Why don't you wear a ruff? . . . Why don't you wear a farthingale? . . . Why do you always ride about the country instead of sitting at home?"

Then sometimes she would change her tone and ask: "Do

you think Kit Oxenbrigge will marry you? . . . Hath he asked your father for you yet? . . . Doth he find you fair in that dirty parlet and brushing gown? . . . Have you heard the new song:

> "But I'll have one that's pretty,
>   Her cheeks of scarlet dye,
> For to breed my delight,
>   When that I lie her by."

And sometimes she would suddenly fly out like a vixen, calling Catherine angry, ugly names—clown, mutton, malkin—and strike at her with her hard little white hands, even before her woman.

"'Tis her age," Madge Piers, her woman, would say; "her planet is combust, as must happen to every woman between forty and fifty, making the times bad. The best physic to take is garlic tea, or a posset of mullein picked under the moon, but my lady won't touch neither."

Catherine, too, tried to tell herself that it was her mother's age, and that she was afraid because of that, and because one day she herself must come to it—that evil time when the ruling planet is combust and the house of a woman's body set alight. But in her heart she knew that neither her own fear nor her mother's anger were because of this. Her mother was angry because she loved Kit Oxenbrigge, and feared that one day he might marry Catherine. She loved him—her house was alight for him . . . Had he entered that house? The thought shook Catherine's body like a sickness.

There was another thought nearly as bad—had anyone else seen the look that she had seen, or watched that hand creep under the ribbons, or heard or dreamed those words? She was not so sharp-eyed that she should see what others were blind to. Her father, she knew, was not a quick or observant man, but there was always someone else about; there was always Robert Douce . . .

So she was back where she started, with Robert Douce's eyes staring at her across the table while his mouth talked with her father about things that had nothing whatever to do with their black, secret look. And she was forced to take refuge where she had taken it before—in her hatred of his and her father's plans for Conster, lashing herself with thoughts of furnaces, hammers, bellows, roarings, rub-a-dubs, waste-hills, cinder-hills, and broken, ravished woods.

3

Early in September the new house at Holly Crouch was finished. On the third day of the month, the ash bough, useful for scaring witches from an empty place, was taken down from the gable.

A week later the wedding-day came and Oliver Harman and Maria Douce were married in Leasan parish church. Afterwards a feast was given at the new house, which was both a marriage feast and a house-warming.

Long tables were laid round the hall, so that all the company could sit down together. It was a large company—the Harmans of Holly Crouch, with their kinsmen from Bodylstret near Pevenseye, all the farm people, and a number of friends, including Squire Alard, with Lady Elisabeth and Catherine, Squire Tuktone with his wife and daughters, Kit Oxenbrigge, and Nicholas Pecksall, parson of the parish.

The bride brought no one but her father and her brother. Sir Philip Sidney was away at the wars, and the Robertsbridge country-side had given no friends to the strangers who had come to make it rich. Young Robert Douce was very like his father, with a long chin, a sallow face and melancholy eyes. It had been planned that he should take charge of Conster Furnace when it was started—he had worked for ten years under his father at Robertsbridge, and knew all the French lore of blast-furnaces, which was changing the Sussex iron industry from a humble, hand-worked affair into an efficient, economical system of power and machinery. Catherine thought he looked stupid, but she did not dislike him as much as she disliked his father, for that very reason.

The Harmans had prepared a truly sumptuous feast for the marriage of their eldest son. There were fricassees, collops, rashers, roast veal and pork, salads of spinach and lettuce, a spitchcock of eels from the Tillingham, and then a second course of game from the Tillingham marshes and poultry from Holly Crouch Yard—with Rhenish wine to drink, and home-brewed ale and sack.

Elisabeth Alard thought it a presumptuous feast for a yeoman to give; except for the preponderance of ale over wine

54

and the absence of devices and a quelque-chose, it might have been given at Conster Manor. She found the company too rough for the food, and though Thomas Harman would have put her at his right hand, she chose rather to sit between Kit Oxenbrigge and Nicholas Pecksall. The bride-pair were opposite her across the table, but she never spoke them a word, preferring to discuss the marriage service with Master Pecksall.

"'Tis a grievous pity," she said, "that the Queen should have taken the old book as it stood, written in such mean language. If instead of consulting the prelates she had consulted the poets—George Peele and Albert Greene, Thomas Kyd or best of all Master Lyly—they would have made a book more worthy of our times and more like to mark the future."

"You would have the Common Prayer written in the style of 'Euphues'?"

"It would be better than as it is written."

"Let me imagine it. Instead of saying 'I, Maria, take thee, Oliver, to be my wedded husband' it would be in this fashion: 'Like as the essences of earth, air, fire and water, cleave to their parts and unite in an indissolubility of elements, like as the cleft peaks of mountains are at the foot in a true singularity of rock, and wandering airs are gathered into one gale, so would I, Maria, cleave, unite and be bound to thee, Oliver, whom I have chosen to be my bridegroom, even as the sun . . . and so forth.' What say you to that, Mistress Maria Harman?"

Maria looked demurely.

"I care not what I say so long as it is in the Protestant religion."

Uneasiness fell over the upper end of the table. The Tuktones sat erect in their seats, and Catherine had to fill her mouth with pie to swallow her fury. Thomas Harman tried to restore the festal atmosphere.

"We wonna' talk of religion to-day since 'tis a matter on which we an't agreed. Let's talk instead of a matter on which we're all as one—Catholics and Protestants, loyal subjects of the Queen. Good folk, fill your jacks and drink the health of our gracious majesty the Queen."

It was a fortunate diversion—the Protestants welcomed any occasion to prove their loyalty, and the Catholics were thankful to have theirs thus publicly proclaimed; while the larger

55

number of those who were neither Catholics nor Protestants, but had fallen into unbelief between two religions, were always glad to shout for the Queen. Tankards were filled and the company rose to drink.

"The Queen!" "The Queen!" "God bless her!" "God save the Queen!"

Alard, Tuktone, Harman, Douce—Protestant, Catholic, Englishman and Frenchman—shouted together.

4

When they had sat down, the health of the bridal pair was proposed by William Luck, being the oldest present. He made a long, rambling speech in which, through age and the decay of his wits, he confused Oliver and Maria with their parents, Thomas and Luce, whose healths he had also drunk at their marriage:

"Seeing as our Master here marries a maid from Brokeslond, he marries wide acres and English blood, and seeing his face is fair and her hair like flax I reckon their children shall be fair as the Queen of England . . ."

Whereat some of the younger and ruder of the company laughed, and the Lady Elisabeth whispered to Oxenbrigge: "Why hath my husband brought me here to listen to yokels raving?"

Old Luck cared nothing for the whispering, which indeed he did not hear, being almost deaf.

"So here's to the bride and bridegroom, and may they be fruitful as the fields of Holly Crouch, and never be troubled with sickness or ghosteses, and live to see their children's children and the true religion back again."

His last words were fortunately lost in the scraping of feet and benches, as the company rose to drink.

"Long life to the bride and bridegroom!" "Long life and many children." "A fine boy this day nine-month." "Fruitful as the fields."

When they had sat down, Nicholas Pecksall stood up to toast Thomas Harman and wish prosperity to the new house; and after him it was Squire Alard's turn to call the health of the bride's father Mounseer Robert Douce.

"Till now our country-side hath owed its wealth to the farms—we have grown good wheat and oats and barley, and now that the laws on hop-growing have been repealed, we're like to grow good hops. Wool an't what it was. I can remember a time when a man counted his money by his fleeces. Other ways pay better now, and some ways 'ull pay better still. I'm talking of iron. There's been ironworks around here since Roman times, but never a chance of their making anyone rich till two things came together—ordnance and blast furnaces. There was never much use for iron when it was wanted only for plough-shares; but when it comes to cannon—by Mary-gipsy! you can't go using the same cannon ball over again. So long as wars shall last there'll be no end to the use of iron. I wöan't speak of this new craze for gates and railings, as some döan't hold with it, but it means good fortune for the iron-masters. With the old handworked bellows they could never have done it, but now we've found the use of water-power for the hammers, and new ways of smelting . . . that's what my friend, the bride's father, Mounseer Douce, hath come to teach us. He had his own blast-furnace over in France, till the times grew too hard for his religion—though I wöan't speak of that, seeing we've so many different notions here; then he came to this country and hath been clerk of the works to the Sidneys at Robertsbridge for a dunnamany years. He hath settled among us and hath his letters of denisation. He will make us all rich, not only at Robertsbridge but at Leasan. At his good advice I shall blow a furnace at Conster, and his son, young Master Robert, shall be my clerk of the works. Soon around here we'll be an iron country, the same as at Wadhurst and at Ashburnham and at Robertsbridge. Our earth is as full of good iron, and we have acres and miles of forest to draw on for timber. The farms will continue to prosper—döan't think I'm standing up to speak against the farms—but in days to come this country-side 'ull be richer than farms could ever make it. Think of the work there'll be, not only for the iron-workers but for the foresters, the carters, the carriers and a dunnamany more; think of the money there'll be to spend on corn and wool and hops—and stand up with me to drink long life to the bride's father, Mounseer Robert Douce, and to the furnace he's going to set up at Conster."

A number of new things seemed to be starting on this day—a new house for the Harman family, a new life for the bride and bridegroom, a new industry for the neighbourhood . . .

the company, which had drunk well, felt merry and excited at the thought of all these new things. There were hurrays and hulloos, and somebody called for dancing.

5

The feast had now lasted three hours, and everyone was glad to rise from the tables, and push them back against the walls to make room for dancing. One of the farm men could play the recorder and another had a gittern; they were told to fetch them and play a jig.

Elisabeth Alard yawned, standing apart with Oxenbrigge.

"Am I bound to stay here till the bride goes to bed?"

"No doubt I can take you home when you've danced a little. You must dance a little first with your husband. Then you may go to bed before the bride."

"I said not I would go to bed."

"But I say you will go to bed."

"Hush! What is it to you if I go to bed or not? Hush! This is horrid music."

> " 'Pipe merry Annot,
>   Trilla, trilla, trillarie'

a fine tune for a tarbox to bump his wench about."

"Indeed I can't stay here, watching clowns dance to such a din."

"You must dance with your husband."

"Not a jig. Surely no one expects me to dance a jig. I'll dance a galliard if the fools can play it."

Oxenbrigge went up to the musicians, who told him they could play a galliard very well. He came back grinning.

"There's no help for it. You must dance with your husband."

"Then you must dance with Kate."

"I'd sooner watch you dance."

"With my husband?"

"I shall see only you."

He bent his dark face to hers, and his eyes were like the eyes of a hawk above her. Catherine saw them standing and looking at each other, and her cheeks burned, while the rest of her body felt cold. The next minute he came up to her and asked her to dance. She was so surprised that she could not answer.

He repeated his request.

"Thank 'ee. I cannot dance."

The words came out of her coldness in a sudden heat. She scarcely knew why she had said them, nor why she was hot and cold.

"But I've seen you dance."

"Not to-night," she said thickly, and turned away.

She was trembling and disturbed. For the first time she smelt craft in him towards her. Was he using her as a decoy for gossip? Even now she could not believe that he needed any decoy. Disappointment was making her superstitious, a chaser after looks and tones. She had best not think at all about Oxenbrigge . . . and now she couldn't dance, because she had told him that she couldn't, and one of the Harmans would be sure to ask her, or Richard Tuktone . . . The jig had given place to a galliard, and most of the country dancers and farm servants had dropped out, leaving the floor to their betters, who alone could tread such a measure. She saw her father lead out her mother, and Richard Tuktone take Maria Harman—which Catherine thought a supererogation of courtesy, remembering what she had said to his face at table . . . Oliver Harman came forward to invite Catherine, but she shook her head, smiling sadly.

"Thank 'ee, but I'm tired to-night."

Her voice was low, and her body seemed to droop against the wall. He pitied her, and fetched her a stool, before going to lead out Agnes Tuktone.

A number of people stood against the wall, among them Nicholas Pecksall, who could tread a galliard as well as anyone. When he saw Catherine sitting down, he came up to her.

"Why don't you dance?"

"Why don't you?"

He looked down at his cassock.

"What would Squire Tuktone say to see a priest dance?"

"I know not. But he must have seen a parson dance before this."

"So you think to-day I'm not a priest?"

"Surelye, you're here as parson of the parish. Maria Douce wouldn't go before a priest to be married."

"Be not so pert with me, Kate. I came here to be happy; and I'll dance if you'll stand up with me."

She shook her head.

"No, no—I've refused two partners. Likewise it would offend Squire Tuktone."

"You've said it would not offend him—he's well used to seeing parsons dance."

"But not to seeing Catholics dance with parsons."

He coloured, and drew back from her.

"Why do you frump me? And if you won't dance with me and won't talk kindly, I'll go home. I have prayers to read."

"Common Prayers?"

He bowed, and left her.

She felt bruised. It seemed to her now as if he boasted his apostasy, then as if she had driven him out of a better mood into such boasting. She could not tell if he were priest or parson—sometimes he appeared to her as one and sometimes as the other. He was false as both.

Then she looked up, and saw him dancing with Margery Harman . . . He must have done it to affront her, to defy her, after all she had said . . . And that was what he was, then—the dancing parson at a wedding. Well, she was glad to know at last.

She felt more miserable than ever, and sat for a while staring at the room through a fog of tears. Then old William Luck came up, a little mazed and grinning after all the ale, to pour into her ear a shambling tale of some ghosts he had seen. "Tur'ble old ghosteses, tur'ble old ghosteses, and all wud writing on their faces. I wur up in a dream at Wyleshammes Crouch, and there they stood in a row around the smithy, all tall and lean, wud white heads shining through wud light, and writing on 'em. I'm lost to think what it may mean."

Catherine did not like hearing about ghosts, knowing how many there were about in the country round Conster, and like to be more, for lack of holy water and the right prayers. But she was too good natured to drive the old man away, and sat there suffering him and blinking her tears till suddenly the dance ceased. The couples scattered from the floor, and the next minute somebody cried for a jig.

"A jig! a jig! . . . . a hey!—hey! hey!"

The recorder and the gittern broke into a jolly, tumbling

tune, and all the farm servants and country people ran out on the floor. Everyone wanted to dance, because only a few had been able to dance the galliard. A merry girl seized hold of old William and dragged him among the dancers—"See my fancy! see my doxy!" Soon they were all kicking and jigging, and through the whirl of colours and dust Catherine saw her mother go out of the room, accompanied by Oxenbrigge.

For a moment she felt cold again. Why were they sneaking together like that? Where was her father? She caught sight of him talking to Robert Douce, and it seemed, though she could not see him clearly through the crowd, that the Frenchman watched the door. She half stood up—she would go home too . . . it was her duty to her mother . . . Then suddenly she came to herself. Surely there was nothing more natural than that her ladyship should tire of such a company, and that, since her husband would never tire of it, Oxenbrigge should escort her home. As if to confirm this happier mood, the Squire came up and spoke to her.

"Thy mother's tired, and I've sent her home. Wilt dance with me, Pug?"

She realized that now Oxenbrigge had left she could dance, and at once the last of her unhappiness was gone. She sprang to her feet, and with a whoop was on the floor, her silken skirts held up to her knees, her long legs flying in their crimson stockings. She loved to dance, and in her new relief was content to dance with her father. The Squire liked nothing better than a jig, and for half an hour they danced together. Then he led out Petronill, the youngest Harman girl, while Catherine was partnered by Oliver Harman. She saw Nicholas Pecksall with his eyes upon her, and she was glad that he should see her dance—she danced all the higher for the sight of him there, watching and wondering.

Her partner complimented her on her recovery.

"I'm glad to see you've gotten back your dancing feet."

"I was all lumperdee clumperdee after the eel pie. I'm uncommon fond of eel pie, and maybe I ate too much of it. I'm light again now."

"Light as a rail," he said as he swung her round.

The day was gone, and the torches were kindled in the sconces on the wall. The light of the room changed from pearl to a smoky topaz, as the air grew thick with the smoke of the torches; and in that cloudy gold the dancers jigged to and fro, men and girls with hot, sweating faces, tumbled hair and many-coloured clothes. On and on went the gittern and the recorder, playing jigs and heys and rigadoons, thrumming and fluting . . . thrumpledum, thrumpledum, thrumpledum, thrum . . . toodleloodle poop, toodleloodle poop . . . and on and on and on . . .

At last there was a movement at the other end of the room. The bride was going to bed. Luce Harman and her daughters went with her, but would allow no one else, and it was understood that when the bridegroom's summons came, he would go up alone. Squire Alard was disappointed, as he had looked forward to a merry company in the bridal room; but Catherine was glad. She had no wish to see Maria Douce (as she still thought of her) sitting up among her brave new sheets and pillows in her brave new marriage bed, waiting in mingled bashfulness and pride for the love that might never come to some people. She would rather dance till she was tired and know that she would find sleep at home—dance with her father, and with farmers' sons who could never wed her . . . on and on and on . . . jig-a-jig-a-jig . . . dancing high to the tune of a gittern and a recorder . . . thrumpledum, thrumpledum, thrumpledum, thrumpledum . . . toodleloodle poop.

Chapter Five

A FEW days later Catherine was consoled for the sad opening of the new house. She knew now that it had been sad, in spite of all the dancing and gaiety. It had been sad with forebodings and uneasinesses, with whispers and glances and the silent opening and shutting of doors . . . with the shadow of a dancing Parson.

Then a week later she ventured to Fuggesbroke, and Agnes Tuktone told her that a priest was coming at last. They had heard—in that mysterious way the family heard their news, the process of which was never revealed to Catherine—that a Father Francis Edwards was at West Rooting and would shortly travel eastward. The exact date of his arrival was uncertain, but as soon as they knew it they would inform Thomas

Harman. Squire Tuktone had seen him and had found in him a true desire to be reconciled.

Her mother of course, said Agnes, was in agonies of fear, but her father would insist that they were fortunate and must share their fortune. Agnes was a little ashamed of her mother, and pleaded in her excuse that she had never recovered from the beating up of the family a year ago—a catastrophe which the young people had taken more calmly than their elders.

"My father was saved by his prayers, but he was grievously troubled—fearing for us all and what would befall us. There's talk now of our going to live at Colespore. I should like it above all things, for Fuggesbroke is a sad place now the best of our furniture is gone. But my mother can't bear to leave her rooms, though I tell her 'twould be safer for us all if the Manor house were empty, and maybe reputed haunted, so that when a priest came, any that saw or heard aught uncouth might think it was ghostes."

Catherine asked her who could come in from the country-side besides herself and Harman.

"The folk at Piramannys Garden and the yeoman of El-lede and Old Mother Eggulsden of Stynts—such as have al-ways come to us. My mother is used to those. The only one she fears is Thomas Harman."

"Poor old Tom! All he asks is to make peace."

"Aye. He told my father that his sickness grows on him and will not be stayed by mullein or poke-root. My father saith 'twould be sin to refuse him, for he is near death, and he saith there's nothing in the Common Prayer to die on."

"Then let him die on the Mass—so long as we die not of his dying on it. . . . Ha! Ha! Ha!" and Kate laughed her great ploughboy laugh.

She was in high spirits because of Agnes Tuktone's news. The shadows seemed lifted from her mind—the shadows of slipping and touching . . . the shadow of a dancing Parson . . . Riding from Fuggesbroke, she decided to go home by way of Leasan Parsonage. When at last she had seen Master Nicholas she had spoken saucily and regrettably, and now she felt that she must see him again to make peace. Her light heart seemed to bounce her towards him.

The same light heart urged her to stop on her way and visit the house known as Piramannys Garden, then the farmstead

63

of Ellede, and the cottage at Stynts, where lived an old woman said by some to be a witch, because she had wondrously survived the frozen winter of '82, when there was neither corn nor meat for poor people. She told no secrets, but it pleased her to talk of their common religion, full as she was of the hope of their common Table.

"Times have not been the same," said the old farmer of Ellede, "since religion was made an Act of Parliament. The country's twice as full of ghosteses and beggars, and when our cows sicken they mun die, there being no holy friar to say the Principio for them. I lost three cows last winter, all for want of the Principio."

"And our churches no better than our barns," said his wife, "with all the holy colours taken away and the holy saints, and English read out in them, same you and me 'ud be talking to each other in the yard."

At Stynts, the old woman showed Catherine her chaplet, which she kept hidden in a sack of meal, and told her that never since religion was taken away had she missed her prayers.

"And many's the dream I've had of holy ones telling me that if I will but pray for it religion will come back again. But not for many years, they say, as 'tis gone uncommon far. . . . Howsumdever, they tell me I shan't die without the host. I shall die houselled and shriven, so as I can go on praying."

"You think maybe that a priest will come to Fuggesbroke?"

"My priest comes from Conster."

She spoke so certainly that Catherine was amazed.

"How can he come from Conster?"

Mother Eggulsden shook her head and repeated:

"He comes from Conster."

Catherine had a sudden, lovely thought.

"Tell me . . . might it be . . . Have you been told his name?"

But the old woman had not been told his name.

2

Nicholas Pecksall was the son of an earlier Parish Priest of Leasan. Born under King Harry, he had been bred up as a Priest's son, custom allowing what authority forbade. His father had ridden the ecclesiastical waves into Queen Marie's

64

reign. He had watched the Pope go with a detached regret, the monasteries go with satisfaction—for he had never been on good terms with the monks in his neighbourhood, whom he held to be envious of his wife and other comforts, and who had certainly treated him to a measure of denunciation.

Later on he fell in agreeably with Cranmer's changes, and had read from both the Prayer Books before they disappeared under the returning tide. It was that returning tide which washed him away to Holland, out of his comfortable stall in Canterbury Cathedral where Cranmer himself had placed him. It threatened a bigger storm than any there had yet been in his life, and he could not know that storm would be so brief. Anyway, he died before it subsided—died believing England a Papist country, but comforted by the thought that the monks had not got back to Battle Abbey, nor were likely to get there in spite of the Queen's religion.

His son Nicholas had not followed his father to Holland. The Queen's accession found him at Oxford; he had never cared for Protestantism, and on this new change turned over wholeheartedly to the Catholic Church. Two years later he was ordained by Cardinal Pole, and made Parish Priest of Leasan, where he had been born and bred.

All his life he had loved the place and it had been his ambition to return there. Now he was scarcely back when the Queen died, and Queen Bess succeeded her. At first he did not think that would mean any serious changes—everyone said the new Queen disliked the Protestants, and in spite of certain utterances and tendencies was really a Catholic at heart. Even after the departure of the Catholic hierarchy and the appointment of Matthew Parker as Archbishop of Canterbury, he still told himself—as so many parish clergy told themselves—that the Queen had been overridden, that to keep her throne she had consented to the Protestant Lords, but would work for the old religion to come back.

Like many of the parish clergy, he continued to say Mass secretly, using the Common Prayer for outward show. It was not till Act had piled on Act and persecution succeeded to prescription that he knew that all was lost—and by that time he was lost too. His roots were sunk in the Sussex earth. It was easier to forsake Rome than Leasan—in his practice, that is to say, for in his heart he still kept the old beliefs, and

65

regarded the reformers, whether from Augsburg or Geneva, as sorry pedants, led astray by a wondrous little learning.

He himself was a man well learned in science and philosophy, of a studious, contemplative cast of mind, loving peace and kindness, also the homely tasks and pleasures of country life. The persecutions of the Protestants troubled him scarcely more than the strugglings and schemings of the Catholics. If only they would stop provoking one another, he said, there would be a better chance for religion in the country. Religion was a plant that must be allowed to grow—all these uprootings and replantings would end in making the land a pagan waste. He had no particular love for the wild rye the last lot of Bishops had sown, but it was keeping the land green, so let it grow. He told himself that he was keeping rather than scattering religion by remaining at Leasan, and comforted himself for the injuries his words and actions did to his beliefs by reading learned books and growing roses.

This particular evening found him in his arbour, eating a supper of fruit and bread, for the September air was soft and spiced with burning leaves.

"Sup with me, Kate—you're all I lack for a fine evening," he said as she came up the garden.

His voice sounded a little forced. He was uncertain what her mood would be, for they had last met at Noll Harman's wedding, and there she had been curst as a wasp. But when she came near he saw that she looked young and gay. The dragged look that he had lately seen on her was gone. She held out her hand, and a grin broke into her face like a flash of snow.

He was surprised to find her so suddenly kind to him.

"So you will sup with me?" he said as she sat down.

"I'll bite an apple, but I mun sup at home. My mother scolds if I ain't back by dark."

"Where have you been all day?"

"At Fuggesbroke."

Her kindness was spoilt.

"Catherine, must you go there?"

"Aye, and back again."

She laughed loudly at him like a boy. He saw that she was in wild spirits, something more than in a happy mood. What was there at Fuggesbroke that could have changed her so from the glum girl he had seen at Harman's wedding? Then suddenly he knew. . . . He could guess the sort of happiness she would find at Fuggesbroke—the only possible sort she could ever find among those sour, ridden folk who could give her neither kind kisses nor good ale. It was just like Kate to laugh and bounce because of the Mass . . .

"They have a priest?—or a priest is coming?"

"Why should you say that?"

"Because Fuggesbroke hath made you happy, and I can think of nothing there in the way of good cheer or pleasant wit, so I am driven to think that the cause of your joy is spiritual."

She pursed up her mouth, but the laughter brimmed up in her eyes. She was more like a schoolboy than the stale maid her fate had decreed.

"Catherine, you're mad if you hear Mass again at Fuggesbroke."

"Why so?"

"Why so? Surely you are not so simple as to need telling that."

"But you know this an't the first time I've heard Mass at Fuggesbroke."

"And have I never warned you? Let that be. Happily you weren't in any great danger. But now—two months after the Grand Armada, when all the country's in arms against the Pope . . . if you're found there will be no mercy for you, be you seven times your father's daughter. Kate, promise me you won't do this mad thing."

"I'll promise you näun."

" 'Nothing,' child or 'naught'—have you forgot I once taught you to speak the English tongue? But you provoke me. What am I to do? Richard Tuktone is a villain to expose you to such danger. My God! you're as mad as the moon."

"If you were saying Mass at Leasan I shouldn't be hearing it at Fuggesbroke."

"That's true. And if the Pope's religion were back in England no one would be hanged for following it. I taught you logic as well as English, and now it seems you remember as much of one as of t'other. But, Kate, tell me—when is this to be?"

"I know not yet."

67

"But soon."

"Aye, I trust so. And mind—it was you who first told me we couldn't live without the Mass. I haven't forgotten that."

"You remember as much of my teaching as pleases you. That, I reckon, is ever the fate of Domines. But, Kate, let's have done with jesting, and talk solemnly on a solemn matter. I've always feared for you at Fuggesbroke, but this is seven times more dangerous. Do you never think at all? Can't you see a difference between now and then? If you're found—and there are more spies about than ever—you'll be reckoned with Tuktone and arraigned for harbouring—that means high treason and hanging . . . the best you can hope is to die in prison . . . Oh, Kate, for God's sake, let me persuade you."

His vehemence surprised her. He had always known of her going to Mass at Fuggesbroke, and she had not expected his opposition to be so much fanned up by recent events, which she had scarcely thought of once the bonfires had died down. She thought he made too much of the danger, and anyway she would not be moved by it.

"I reckon I'd be a tur'ble, miserable coward if I let myself be scared when there's such a fine hope for all of us."

"Who's 'all of us'?"

"The folk around here—Tuktone and many more."

"Not many, Kate. There's not many folk round here who'd walk half a mile to get the Pope back again. I know that most of our people think kindly of the old faith and miss what they used to find in our churches, but no one truly cares, and quite a number have forgotten the doctrine they used to know and have filled their heads with superstition."

"And who's to blame for that?"

"You would say that I am. But, dear child, one reason why I don't fall in with your plots is that I would preserve some sort of religion for our people."

She stared at him incredulously.

"You can't know what I know," he continued. "You have not lived through four changes of religion."

"You needn't have changed each time with it."

"I did not change—my heart hath never changed; though I'll agree that my outward practice hath varied somewhat. But even so I said Mass in the midst of Archbishop Parker's visitations . . . Nosey Parker Parker we clergy used to call him,

for his nose was everywhere, sniffing out neglect or heresy or
simony or superstition. I said Mass till I knew the old religion
would never come back again—then I thought it well to do
what I could with the new."

"If only a thousand Masses could be said all over England
in one day, the Pope 'ud be back the next."

" 'If only'—such a little thing as that. You're modest, Kate,
and rational."

She could not answer irony, but frowned as it bit her.

"Some day it will be done," she said sullenly.

"Never, child—not now, after this last affair of the Armada.
That pious Spanish gesture settled religion in this country
for ever. Doubtless many folk still think well of the old faith,
but they begin to feel scared about the Pope. He no longer
means Holy Church to them, but foreign cogging and slavery.
If King Philip meant to do more than punish our pirates for
their raids on the Spanish Main, he erred, for instead of bringing back the Pope to these shores he hath shut him out for
ever."

"I can't believe it."

"I'm sure of it, and I'm likewise sure that my duty to my
flock is not to deceive them with tales or stuff them with false
hopes, but to gather together for them such fragments of religion as remain in this poor country. My story is their story
too."

"They an't all priests' bastards," she snapped in her pain.

"I'm not a bastard," he said quietly. "But I'm a man who
hath had his religion changed four times by Act of Parliament.
It is the same with the folk here, and can you wonder if their
poor heads are turning round? I tell you, if we go on staggering
and changing we'll end no better than Turks and Blackamoors.
Our only chance is some sort of settlement, and I for one refuse to do anything to upset matters again. The present Es-
tablishment is not what I should choose, but I believe that
something can be made of it. There's a foundation to build
on. The Book of Common Prayer is full of loopholes and es-
capes; we may be able to build up some sort of religion out of
it. But we'll build nothing out of chaos . . ."

He stopped suddenly, for he saw that Catherine was in
tears.

"Kate! . . . my child! . . . what have I said?"

She sobbed brokenly, turned away from him, her head hidden in the crook of her arm.

"You mustn't take me so hard," he said gently. "I'm only trying to persuade you for your good."

"To—to persuade me . . . that—that life an't worth living. That's all your persuasion. If religion's dead, then I mun die too."

He felt suddenly angry with her.

"Why do you always rave so? Are you quite without reason?"

"I speak reasonable truth. If the old religion's gone, then I'd better die—for what have I to live for?"

"You're mad," he repeated, "as mad as the moon."

"Let me be, then. I'd sooner lose my mortal wits than my immortal soul."

He saw that all his talk had persuaded her to nothing. Her heart, empty of so much that should have filled it, was like a drum beating martial music. He could as well have persuaded the army of the Netherlands. She was set on her own ruin, and he would never reason her out of it. He must find other means for her safety.

After a moment's silence, during which his mind moved resolutely, he spoke in another voice.

"Dear Kate, let us not be for ever wrangling and threaping each other. We are good friends—let us behave as friends and eat our supper together without fantastical disputes. Forget what I have said and I will forget some words of yours that have injured me."

"I meant not to injure you," she mumbled, wiping the tears from her face.

"Think no more of it. We all insult and injure one another when our theological passions are stirred. You and I should have lived in a less contentious age; happily we yet may live in it."

"I hope not."

"You love contention?"

"Nay, I love it not, but I know your uncontentious age for an age of death. Some souls may find their graves before their bodies."

"Not yours and mine. They will only pass out of a bad world of contention into a pleasant paradise of friendly intercourse.

Let us now anticipate that golden age and talk of books."

"Books! I never read any."

"Have you not read the 'History of Friar Bacon and Friar Bungay' that I lent you before Midsummer? Nor 'Pandora'? nor 'Friar Rush'? nor 'The Tragedy of Feerex and Porrex'? all of which you have now in your home, though they are mine. Miserable girl!"

He had won a smile from her at last, and soon her teeth were in her apple as he made a mock of scolding her.

3

On an evening in the third week of September, when the year was losing the hard, gay colours of summer and growing rich and troubled and dim, a lad came over to Conster from Fuggesbroke, bringing Catherine Alard a word from Agnes Tuktone. A pedlar had visited the house with some delightful wares. Would she ride over and see them?

Catherine, pleasantly excited, sent for her horse to be brought round. Agnes' message might, and probably did, mean more than appeared. The summons came each time in a different guise. She could not tell . . . and even if the pedlar were no more than he seemed, he would not come amiss, for she was simple enough still to find pleasure in ribbons and billiments on a tray.

She had some difficulty in starting. Her mother wanted a groom to go with her.

"The way you ride about alone is most unseemly. Some day you will have a misfortune—you will be ravished. I hear that there's a number of rascals on the road."

"I an't afraid"—Catherine tossed her head—"I reckon that if anything of that sort 'ud been coming to me it 'ud have come by now."

"It may come yet—and what will you do *then* for a husband?"

Catherine felt the sword between them. She stood looking at her mother, and then the hope that had been in her since Agnes' message came, made a sudden tenderness in her heart. She stooped and kissed her.

"Love me, Mother—for I love you."

Elisabeth Alard was startled. For a moment something hurt her, then she thrust it aside. She said:

"Why don't you use civit and musk? You smell of sweat."

Catherine turned from her and mounted her horse. Tears were burning and blinding her eyes. As she shook the reins her mother called:

"When will you be back?"

"Not till cockshut. I shall sup at Fuggesbroke."

She cantered off, closing her heart.

Starvencrow Hill was brown and gold and red, with the bracken and the gorse and the fruit of the thorn. There had been little rain or dew, and the ground was firm under the hoofs of Ball, her horse. She would not follow the road, but set him at the hill, galloping up to the hedges of Holly Crouch, and then round Dodyland Shaw to the lane by Colespore. Down the hill . . . and there was Fuggesbroke on the slope above her, looking upon the stream—Fuggesbroke, no longer merely a despoiled, impoverished Manor house but the casket of salvation, the treasury of the key and of the gold. O gloria! She could forget that her mother did not love her any more.

The Tuktone girls, Agnes, Margaret, and Susanna, were waiting for her. The pedlar was in the solar with their parents. He sat on a wooden stool, a small, slight, delicate-looking man; beside him was his tray, bright with ribbons and lace and gingerbread. Round him clustered the Squire, his wife, his sons and daughters and his four maidservants—a more cheerful family than Catherine had ever seen at Fuggesbroke. As she looked round at them all, she understood. She could scarcely speak—her voice choked her as, dropping on one knee, she mumbled: "Bless me, Father!"

"Beware!" cried Mary Tuktone, looking anxiously at the windows. But no one was there to see the pedlar give his blessing.

"Sit down, Catherine," said Richard Tuktone. "Our friend here hath merchandise for you."

"Merchandise?"

She stared in some perplexity at the little tray with its cheap, common objects.

"Nay, it is not merchandise, since I ask no price. Take it, Mistress, with my good will."

She saw that he was holding her out a letter.

"What is that? Who can have written to me?"

"Open it and see. You love the writer."

"Nay, I've no need——"

She began to tremble. Certainly she had no need to break the seal—the characters of the address were enough to show her who had written it. She held in her hand her first, her only, letter from her brother Simon.

For a moment joy made her dumb, then a crowd of questions came stammering to her lips.

"Oh, Sir, tell me . . . pray . . . have you seen him? Did he give it to you? Is he well?"

"Aye, he is well, and I have seen him, and he gave me this letter with his own hand, knowing that I should reach England some time ahead of him."

"Ahead . . . then he is coming?"

"Happily even now he is on his way. When I last saw him it was at the Church of Santa Maria in Vallicella, where he had gone, as I had, to ask the blessing of Father Philip Neri, whose custom is to bless the English priests as they set out for death in their own country. He loves all young men, especially those appointed to die early in such a manner."

Catherine did not hear him. While he spoke she had torn open the letter and now was reading it, frowning a little at the long words. At first the characters seemed to swim in the sea of her excited tears—then she saw her own name, and soon had spelled out the rest, for it was short. When she had read it she slipped it into her bosom.

"What says he, Kate?" asked Agnes.

"That he reckons to set out in a few days. He will cross Italy and France, and will go to some port whence he can take ship for Chichester. Then he will come presently to Conster. Oh, I can scarce believe it . . . I knew not even that he was priested."

"It is good news for us all," said Richard Tuktone. "Maybe he will say Mass for us at Fuggesbroke."

"'At that he will for sure!" cried Kate.

"And now," said Tuktone, "we must talk of tomorrow. What time do you wish us here, Sir?"

"You have told me there is a Protestant to be reconciled."

"Scarce a Protestant—I reckon him no worse than a conformer."

"You know him?—you trust him?"

Sitting there, opposite the priest, Catherine noticed he looked very ill. His face was pale and moist, and his hands fumbled continually. She thought that maybe he had been in prison.

This would account for his extreme fearfulness. She had met lion-hearted priests at Fuggesbroke—Thomas Pilchard, John Oven, and others like them, men who were ready for all dangers, who would never have seen any obstacle to the reconciling of a heretic. But Father Francis Edwards seemed as scared as Mary Tuktone of poor Thomas Harman, and into the midst of her husband's vindication of him came his wife crying:

"You do well to mistrust him, Sir. His son is married to the daughter of a Protestant spy."

"A spy!—are you sure of it? Who is he? and where is he now?"

"Nay! nay! he is no spy," cried Richard Tuktone and Catherine in one breath but with varying minds. Tuktone was sure that Robert Douce was no spy, merely one of a number of foreign fugitives come to spoil the country. Catherine, on the other hand, felt sure he was a spy, but also felt sure that she and Harman and Tuktone and them all would be more than a match for him.

In the end the Squire's arguments prevailed over his lady's, by virtue of the Priest's office, which forbade him to refuse a penitent even at the cost of his life.

"Let him come then. God will preserve us if we do His will. How many do you reckon beside him from without?"

"Maybe half a score."

Catherine wondered if he would also protest at these, but the mantle of his pastoral zeal covered them too. His tired, hollow eyes grew brighter with the love of souls.

"I'm glad indeed. It comforts my heart to think how our faith hath kept alive all these years in the midst of death."

"Would that we had more than half a score," said Richard Tuktone. "What's half a score in a neighbourhood of six or seven hundred?"

"The rest, I suppose, conform?"

"As much as they must. But the parish churches are nearly empty. Folk don't like 'em stripped and bare, and most of

74

'em are superstitious about speaking to God in their own tongue."

"If a priest were able to stay any time in these parts, doubtless he would find that nine-tenths of the people are Catholic at heart."

"Not now—remember there's a generation born and grown up without the Faith. I doubt, though, if they've anything much in its place."

"So that when we come back we find the house swept and garnished"—his eyes were blazing now. "Let's take the parable in the manner of our enemies and say our holy Father is the strong man armed who is turned out of his castle, and returns with seven others more wicked than himself—with seven others more holy than himself, even the seven archangels armed in power and might."

A violent fit of coughing interrupted him, and Catherine suddenly guessed he was in a decline.

"This is perilous talk," said Mary Tuktone. "Let's change it and go to our supper. It is ready now in the hall."

They went into the hall and sat down to a plain meal of bread and cheese and salad, washed down with the poorest ale. To Catherine it was a kind of Last Supper, for before she ate again she would visit Mount Calvary, she would see her Lord die upon the Cross and rise again. It was more than a year since she had been shriven or had heard Mass, and now she could scarcely believe that her fast was ended. Her soul was thin—it sorely needed food from heaven . . . "And in the strength of the angel's food Elias went forty days and forty nights" . . . Catherine might have to go forty weeks or forty months . . . No matter—the angel's food would sustain her as it had sustained Elias. It was her own fault that her soul was thin—it was like her body, always galloping about alone. . . .

These thoughts kept her grave and silent during the meal, and directly it was over she rose to go. The last appointment had been made. Mass would be said at four o'clock, and she must be back at Fuggesbroke by half-past three. She would have to walk, for it would be difficult to get her horse from the stable, and apart from that she must go more softly than on iron hoofs . . . She said good-bye to the Tuktones; it was to be only a few hours' parting.

"Good-bye," said Richard Tuktone. "We shall meet again in Paradise."

Her face darkened; she did not for a moment understand him.

"A Paradise on earth," he said, laughing. "A Paradise in an upper room."

She grasped his meaning, but could not share his mirth.

4

As soon as she was on horseback she lost her solemnity. The dusk had fallen, though supper had been early, for the days were drawing in. The sweet air, the comfort of her meal, the strong movement of Ball under her, made her forget both the shadow of Mount Calvary and the other shadow that had fallen on her suddenly at the moment of farewell. She sang as she rode.

> "When as the rye reach to the chin,
>   And chop-cherry, chop-cherry ripe within . . ."

At the foot of Starvencrow Hill, the valley was a pool of darkness, for the tide was out, and the tidewaters of the Tillingham were not spread to catch the last pale light.

> "Strawberries swimming in the cream,
>   And schoolboys playing in the stream;
>   Then, O, then, O, then, O, my true love said,
>   Till that time come again
>   She could not live a maid."

Catherine sang in her loud boyish voice, singing louder and louder, because she was afraid. The shadow of Brede Eye, the great tree-covered hill behind Conster, had fallen across the valley and was upon her now as she rode down the hill. Lower in the valley, in the shadows by the stream, she might meet ghosts, or the fair fiends, whom the Leasan folk called Pharisees.

> "Then, O, then, O, then, O, my true love said . . ."

She shut her eyes, trusting her horse to pick his way to the ford. Through her song she could hear the trees whisper and then the sighing of the stream. A branch touched her face and she was nearly out of her saddle . . . She must keep her eyes open and her wits about her.

> "Then, O, then, O, then, O . . ."

Closh-closh-closh . . . They were over the ford and on the grassy, lawned slope below Conster. Music came out to meet her, and for a wild moment she thought the fair fiends were there, then knew the sound of her cousin's lute. No doubt he was playing to her mother in the *privée*. She would not go in to them.

She rode round to the stables and gave up her horse to a groom.

"Is the Squire home?"

"Nay, Mistress. He and Master Douce are at the furnace with lanthorns. Then Master Douce comes back here for to-night."

Lord help us, thought Catherine as she went into the house. Must we never be rid of that man? Now I suppose he will be always here. She was suddenly afraid that he would see her go out in the morning—that he was there for the very purpose, working her father's schemes to suit his own. But she swallowed the fear down, knowing that her plans must go forward in spite of it.

She had had her supper, so she went straight upstairs to her room. As she passed through the hall she noticed that the lute-playing did not come from the *privée*, but from a smaller parlour or bower set apart for her mother's own use. Again she felt fear, and again she drove it out. She must go to bed and sleep, or she would be heavy to-morrow.

Up in her room she found her woman waiting, and immediately sent her away. She wanted no help to pull off her gown and petticoat, and she wanted no one to see her as she opened a chest and took from the lining of a cloak folded there a string of rosary beads. They belonged to Simon—when he went away she had given him hers and he had given her his. They were the only token of her faith that she possessed. Kissing them once for heaven and once for him, she slipped them under her pillow. Then she read his letter again . . . "Dere Kate . . . sweete Kate—my owne sister . . ." The words had written themselves in her heart and she could read them there after the candle was blown out.

She wondered then if she should have shown the letter to her mother, but something within her shrank from going near that parlour where the lute was playing. Even if she stumped, and rattled the door she might catch glances that would soil her peace. . . . Then the next moment she remembered that her parents must know nothing of any letter till Father Edwards was gone—or they might guess how it had come to her. A chill went through her as she thought how near she had been to betraying Fuggesbroke. . . . Her mind was like a cullender, full of great holes for secrets to slip through. Perhaps Mary Tuktone was wise to mistrust her. . . . But she would not think of Mary Tuktone.

She lay on her bed, clasping her beads and seeking her way to sleep. The music did not come so clearly as it used to come from the *privée*, and torment was muffled with its sound . . . love could not torment her now—she was beyond its evil . . . "Then, O, then, O, then, O, my true love said . . ." She could fall peacefully asleep, telling her beads and thinking of her brother . . . twankledum twang . . . she could fall asleep to the distant playing of a lute, to a little plaintive air by Tallys or Tye.

5

When she woke the window was pale with light. Her first thought was that she had slept past the hour, that she would be late for Mass. But the next moment reassured her. Gazing out, she could still see the stars over Starvencrow Hill, hanging above the light, which seemed to rise from some hidden point in the north-west. She wondered what it might be—no doubt some rick ablaze. But she need not trouble yet about the dawn, for the handle of the Plough was tilted high in the firmament, instead of hanging low as it would hang before the sunrise wiped it out. Then somewhere in the house a clock struck one.

She might sleep for another two hours. Custom had taught her to time her sleeping to a minute, and neither care nor excitement could keep from her the healthy sleep that was her long day's due. While she slept the light grew round her, fanning out the stars.

She woke punctually at three o'clock, and was able to dress without a candle. This must be more than a stack fire. Maybe a whole farm was ablaze; maybe a Manor . . . no, no, that was another fear that must be cast out. Her strength would fail if she thought of such a thing; already she could feel her knees shake. Her hands fumbled with loops and strings, and every now and then she trod over to the door and listened, wondering if she should hear Robert Douce's footsteps in the house. . . . Or perhaps he watched in the darkness outside her room, waiting to see her leave it. If so, she knew a trick to mate him with.

There was a window of her room unglazed. She had begged her father to leave it so when he rebuilt the house, for she dreaded being shut up behind glass. It was a small, old-fashioned window, scarcely more than a slit or lancet, but she was able to squeeze through, and then there was only a ten-foot drop to the ground.

The grass was heavy with half-frozen dew, and she knew there would be frost at dawn. She could smell it coming and see it among those stars that the light had still left hanging in the eastern sky—making them dance like candles in a wind. She wondered now if the light might be a portent—a terrible foretelling. Her fear grew deeper than when she had let herself think a Manor burned. Strange thoughts flittered through her head as she climbed up Starvencrow Hill. How slowly one went a-foot!—and in such a light one might be seen. Already it was casting shadows; she could see the shadow of the first hedge of Holly Crouch lying long and dark upon the wild lands, as if cast by some monstrous sunrise. She moved towards the gate creeping softly, her skirts heavy with dew.

Then suddenly her heart leapt, and she almost screamed as she saw a man come out from the shadow of the hedge beside the gate.

"Mistress Kate, don't be scared. 'Tis but Tom Harman."

"Why are you here?"

"I came to look for you—you mun go back at once."

"Go back!"

"Surelye. At once. 'Tis all known about the Mass, and the soldiers have been to Fuggesbroke. You can see the light in the sky."

So her fears had been well grounded. She might have known.

"They started burning it at midnight," he continued, "but I believe they wur there by ten."

"Have you been? Have you seen?"

"No, I haven't been. I dare not, with my share in it. There wur men at arms all around the house, stopping the lanes, so

79

my Dickon told me. I sent un to the Horns as soon as we heard the tale. But there's no getting near the house. Heigh-how! I never thought to be so robbed of my salvation."

"I mun go at once."

"Don't talk so mad, Madam Kate. I tell you the place is all set about wud soldiers."

"I care not. They may take me and welcome. I reckon they've taken Squire Tuktone and Father Edwards. Let 'em take me too."

"No, Madam—you mun't go, for the sake of all of us. Get back to Conster now before you're missed."

He laid a detaining hand upon her arm, but she was as strong as a colt, and shook him off, running from him. He started after her, calling her back, but his sickness made him heavy, and soon he had to stop. She broke through the hedge into the lane, and then ran along it, leaving it just before Haneholt's Wood, to cut across the commonland to Colespore.

6

She was no longer conscious of anything but her body, straining and pumping her to Fuggesbroke. She seemed to have nothing but body left—and luckily her body was all that she needed now. With her elbows at her sides and her neck stretched out, she thudded along the lane, hampered by her long wet skirts, but running on, past Colespore with its sleeping barns, towards the terrible light.

She saw it now, from the corner of the lane—Fuggesbroke, with the flames bursting from its many walls. The stream ran red before it, but she thought the fire looked as if it were dying down: gables stood up against a roofless void and walls stopped short beside a fiery pit. She could see no figures moving, nor did there seem to be any soldiers about.

She slackened her pace a little, and the air seemed to be full of a heavy sighing—at first she thought it was the fire, then knew that it was her own breath. She heard the flames roar as she drew nearer, and with the sound came the terrible smell of a burnt house.

Still there was nobody about. An attempt had been made to break down the bridge across the stream, but it stood firm enough for more than her weight. She crossed it and went up the hill, then turned into the Manor drive. Still there was no one, though she could see the ground was stodged with horses' feet. She could feel the heat of the burning place, and wondered how much nearer she could go.

Then her eyes fell on what at first she had taken for the shadow of Rockers Wood on the field behind the house, and as her mind woke out of its stupor, she realized that the wood could not cast its shadow against the fire . . . this darkness upon the red field must be a group of people . . . soldiers? —no, she could see no armour nor weapons gleaming. They were more likely fugitives from the house.

She hurried towards them, crying as she ran:

" 'Tis Catherine Alard. Is that Squire Tuktone? . . . Agnes! Susanna! Margaret! 'Tis Catherine Alard."

A figure came forward to meet her, followed by warning cries, and the next minute her arms were round a body that trembled convulsively, sobbing and clinging.

"Agnes! Agnes!"

"Kate!"

"I've heard . . . Harman told me . . . What have they done?"

"They've killed my father."

"Oh! . . . Oh! . . ."

She stood, holding Agnes in her arms, sobbing with her, till somebody else came and said:

"Come back, Agnes. Why are you here, Catherine?"

It was Mathew Tuktone, the eldest son. His face was black with soot and smoke and his eyes gleamed redly.

"Why am I here?" faltered Catherine. "I came because Harman told me . . . He said there were soldiers round about, but I saw none."

"You saw none? That's good news."

His voice sounded more friendly.

"Then maybe we can carry Jane to Colespore now," said another voice.

Catherine had joined the group which was gathered under the big oaks of Rockers Wood. It was made up entirely of the Tuktone family and their servants, sitting or standing about. Jane Tuktone lay on a cloak spread on the ground, and beside her knelt Susanna, holding something wrapped in a cloth. Looking closer, Catherine saw the tiny, wrinkled face

81

of a new-born child. Mary Tuktone sat on a tree-stump, pale as a corpse, but with her eyes wide and gazing. Somehow it seemed to Catherine as if this little group of people were not alive at all, but turned to stone.

"Thomas Harman told me—" she began nervously. "He met me as I came to Mass."

As she spoke the last word, she felt her soul wake and cry within her—her soul was crying like a bird whose nest is taken.

"Weep not, dear Kate," said Agnes Tuktone. "You an't to blame for this."

"But I would to God," said Mathew, "that we hadn't listened to you about Harman."

"It an't he who's betrayed you. That I can swear."

"No, but I'll lay it was that spying Huguenot, Robert Douce, and that he heard of it from his daughter."

"She knows näun. How can she know?"

"There hath not always been much prudence," said Mathew Tuktone.

"No," said his brother Giles. "We have trusted too many."

Catherine felt the chill of his words. The family had turned against her, and she felt that, except for Agnes, she had no friend in it now that the Squire was dead. She noticed that Mary Tuktone did not speak at all, nor move, but sat on her tree-stump, staring at Fuggesbroke's embers with eyes that did not ever seem to blink. She would have liked to speak to her, but did not dare. She turned to Agnes instead.

"Agnes, tell me—how could they—dared they—kill your father?"

"Because he sought to defend his own—the holy things which they had found and were defiling. There was a soldier who . . . but I cannot tell you." She gave a few broken sobs, her throat being too sore and choked for more.

"And Father Edwards?"

"He is taken. They are gone with him to Chichester."

At that moment a low cry broke from Jane Tuktone on the grass, and immediately her husband and family gathered round her.

"Surely we can take her now to Colespore."

"Kate says the soldiers are gone."

"Kate, was anyone about Colespore?"

"Not a soul."

"Too scared to move, I reckon. Well, Sinden may put his head out now."

"Anyway we must take her there, or she will die in the field."

"I'll go on ahead and knock up the Sindens. Better not move till I come back."

"I see someone in the field below the house. Maybe 'tis Sinden."

"Or soldiers coming back."

"No—they an't armed or mounted. It is Sinden—I can see him clear, with Nick and Ned. Give 'em a hulloo."

"Have care! Have care!"

"Hulloo!"

"Have care!"

A man's voice answered from near the house, and soon the farmer of Colespore and his sons had joined the group. Preparations were made for carrying Jane to the farm—a hurdle was fetched, and she was laid on it. Catherine stood by, feeling alien and lonely. Nobody seemed to want her or her help; they were all absorbed in one another. She thought that she might have been given a warmer welcome, seeing that she had risked her life to come to them . . . but they thought that their tragedy was all her doing—her "imprudence" . . . They would have it that her plan for Thomas Harman was at the bottom of their trouble. But she could not believe that he had betrayed them, either deliberately or by mistake. Robert Douce had heard of the Mass from some other source—for of course she believed that it was Robert Douce who had betrayed them, though she had argued against it. Robert Douce was what Mathew Tuktone had called him, a Huguenot spy, and it was his business to find out any plan that was toward among the Catholics, and he would have found it out no matter who was or who was not in it. God curse him and rot his eyes! Her anger flamed suddenly and burned itself up. "Father, forgive them"—that should be her spirit. But it was a rare spirit, and seemed now to lie dead with Richard Tuktone.

She saw Margaret and Susanna go up to their mother and try to raise her from where she sat.

"Come away, Mother—come and get warm."

Mary Tuktone spoke at last.

"I am warming myself at a very good fire."

"Mother, come and get warm in bed."

"Did your father send for me?"

"No-o."

"I will go to bed when he comes."

"Mother, mother . . ."

Catherine turned from the sight, and found Agnes Tuktone beside her. The girl said in the little dry voice her sobs had left:

"Oh, Catherine, this will break my heart."

"Poor, sweet Agnes . . ."

"My mother and my father . . . I know not which I suffer in most. My mother most like—and yet she may come back to me; but my father, never. Oh, Kate, the foul deed!"

"It will be punished."

"By whom? The law will take no action, seeing how he was killed; and if my brothers did anything they would only add their lives to his. Besides, he wouldn't ask for vengeance. He was good—is good. Oh, Kate, we must believe he prays for us."

At that moment Kate could believe nothing; her mind was too heavy with grief and horror to fly to heaven after Richard Tuktone. She felt suddenly that she must get away from this family. Their sorrow hurt her too much for her to stay.

"Agnes, I mun go home."

"Won't you walk with us as far as Colespore?"

"No—I mun't wait. I mun go home."

"Lucky Kate to have a home to go to! But it ain't safe for you to run about like this alone at night."

"I'm safe enough, and morning's nearly here. I mun be home by morning."

She hurriedly kissed her friend's cold cheek and slipped away, running like a fox in the shadow of the hedge.

Chapter Six

BEFORE SHE reached home she could smell the dawn, and looking eastward over the spread waters of the Tillingham she could see that the stars were beginning to pale. It was scarcely more than that—a fading in the sky and a scent that troubled her nostrils, yet she could feel the threat of a new day heavy upon the earth. Before it came, she must sleep. She could not face it without some respite of forgetfulness. Her head lolled upon her neck and her limbs ached. It seemed a hundred hours since she had risen for bread and found a stone—a hot, fiery stone such as burning mountains cast forth in the far-away lands where lambs grow as fruit on the trees and weeds cry out beside the water. . . . She was nearly asleep, dreaming as she stumbled up the lawn from the river to the house.

There were lights burning, and when she tried the door she was not surprised to find it open. No doubt the servants were about. But it did not matter. She had no need for secrecy now. She lurched noisily up the stairs, meeting no one.

Her hands groped at the latch of her bedroom door, and she stumbled in, falling upon the bed and lying there with her wet mud-caked skirts spread upon the coverlet, and her hair full of leaves and dew sweeping over her face. She was already asleep.

She woke to find the news of the burning of Fuggesbroke all over the country-side. Her woman was agog with it when she came to dress her.

"Marry-gup, Mistress! What a plight you're in. Let me get you a clean gown."

"No, leave me."

"Let me dress your hair, Mistress Catherine. You look like a Jack-in-the-Green. And what's this I hear? That Fuggesbroke Manor's been beaten up again and burnt up to boot, and Squire Tuktone's run through with a bilbo."

"How heardst thou that?"

"From Nick and the grooms. They all say he was caught in the midst of a plot to kill the Queen, and a seminary priest with him to conjure the devil."

"Hold thy foolish tongue or I'll pull it out. And go get me a livery, for I starve with hunger."

She would not go downstairs till her father and Robert Douce had left for the furnace. She could not face her father till the news was cold, nor could she show him her brother's letter. Indeed, she thought best to burn that in the grate, for now she feared that Robert Douce might find out about his

85

coming and destroy him too. Robert Douce . . . if she were to see just now, that long pale face and those prominent searching eyes, she would scream out all the horror and rage that filled her heart—horror and rage where she had expected love and peace to be planted, flames instead of flowers. Her heart was full of flames, which her tears had only partly extinguished by the time Nan Jordan came back into the room.

The rest of the day passed wretchedly. Though she could avoid her father's questionings she could not avoid her mother's. She must bear those barbed looks and words, feel the very shadows armed between her and her mother. Nor did Oxenbrigge show her any pity.

"So, Kate, your recusant friends were beat up last night. It was a mercy you weren't with them."

"As she would have been," said her mother, "had the soldiers come by day. Kate is all over the country—galloping Kate."

"Maybe she gallops by night as well as by day," said Oxenbrigge, teasing her with his eyes.

"Nay, she sleeps by night," said her mother, "sleeps in her clothes, so her woman tells me."

"How can Nan say so? I was up when she came in."

"But with your hair all wild and full of leaves and your bed as wet as if a fish had slept in it."

Catherine felt her heart beat fast; she tried to speak calmly.

"I was uncommon tired last night. I came in and went straight to bed—you were in your bower."

"And whom had you been rolling with to get yourself in such a state? Nay, hold your tongue. I'm shot of you. Your father shall deal with you."

She picked up a piece of needlework and pointed to Oxenbrigge's lute.

"Play to me, cousin. I am cursed with a daughter."

He picked up his lute, and their eyes, full of amorets, seemed to fly together and meet above the lute like wicked birds.

3

When Kate came home that evening the lute was still playing. It seemed to her as if it had never stopped. All the time she had been riding over the country, trying in vain to ease her soul by bodily exercise, it seemed to her as if that lute had been playing—thrumpledum, thrumpledum, thrumpledum, and on and on and on, while Oxenbrigge's strong, thin hand plucked over the strings, and her mother's crept under the ribbons towards him.

The servants told her that her father was still out, and once more she climbed up to her room, supperless, for grief had soured her stomach and she could not eat. Though she sought solitude she longed for human company. All day she had fought a craving to go to Leasan and sit with Nicholas Pecksall in the parsonage arbour, talking of common, comfortable things. But she would not go—she could not bear his kindness, because she knew that under it would be his triumph, his thankfulness for the rout of Fuggesbroke. His triumph would make his kindness into pity, as watchet is made into purple by a crimson under it. She could not bear his pity, nor its underlying flame—she must face her sorrows alone.

She undressed herself and lay down, closing her eyes and trying not to hear the lute. Thrumpledum, twankledum, thumpledum, twankledum—would it never have done? The tune was meaningless to her now. It no longer rose up and searched the stars. A mere thrumming and twanging came from her mother's bower, and she could not think of the lute as a musical instrument but as a meeting place for wanton eyes and hands.

> "All ye that lovely lovers be,
> Pray you for me."

She no longer loved Oxenbrigge—his lute no longer sang to her, but twanged of false love. He was a low deceiver. . . . Oh, false! false! false! She should tell her father. No, how could she? How could she go to her honest, innocent father and tell him that his cousin made love to his wife? How did she even know that it was true? Her heart was unclean—angry and unclean. *Munda cor meum, Domine.* Oh, God my firmament. . . . Oh all ye holy saints and angels, pray for me—All ye that lovely lovers be, pray you for me. . . . No, what was she saying now? She was falling asleep. I mun sleep, sleep, sleep . . . ye lovely saints and angels . . . ye holy lovers . . . pray for me—pray for me. . . .

She was asleep. She was awake; and the lute was still.

Stillness and darkness seemed to lie over the house together. It must be past midnight. Then to her surprise a clock struck nine. She could not have slept more than a couple of hours.

Why was the house so still? It was early yet for folk to be in bed. Then suddenly she heard her father's voice calling in the great hall.

"Wife, where are you?"

Where was her mother, and where was the lute? She could hear nothing, only footsteps in the hall—two sets of footsteps. Her father and Robert Douce must just have come back from the furnace. . . . The next moment a door opened, and suddenly there were voices—frightened or angry or merry or drunken? She could not be sure. They came from her mother's parlour, not from the hall. Her father must have gone in. There were two men speaking. . . .

While she listened, a great fear took her. The voices were quarrelling—she was sure of that now; and the second man's voice was not Douce's but Oxenbrigge's. She sat up in her bed, trying to hear what was said, but she could not, only knew for sure that they were angry. Sometimes she heard her mother's voice, and that sounded shrill and angry too. On and on and on . . . growing louder . . . and then suddenly a strange and terrible sound, a crash and a groan and a twang. The next moment she knew it was the sound of a lute being broken.

She slid from the bed, flung a cloak over her shift and ran straight away downstairs. In the candlelight of the hall Robert Douce was sitting. She had forgotten all about him, and was startled to see him there, sitting on a bench with his arms folded over his chest, staring into the shadows with a fixed, expressionless face. When he saw her he stood up.

"Mistress Catherine, do not go in."

But she took no notice and, passing him, went straight to her mother's parlour, which was just off a little passage leading from the hall. It looked strangely dim, and she saw that it was lighted only by a candle held in her father's hand. Those in the room had been snuffed out.

In the faint light she could see her mother and Oxenbrigge, standing together opposite her father—on the floor lay Oxenbrigge's lute, smashed to atoms, with the dark, gay ribbons flowing from it like blood. They were all so busy with one another that at first they did not see her in the doorway, where for some moments she stood staring at a mother she had never seen before—a mother flushed and tumbled, with big, terrified eyes, and terrified fingers that groped with the fastenings of her gown. Oxenbrigge was changed too—he had lost his clean, hawk-like air, his hair was rough and his clothes were untidy. Catherine stared and suddenly understood. Her feet felt like roots in the ground, and she could not move when her mother screamed at her: "Go! go!"

Then her father turned round.

"Kate, get out o' this!"

At last she was able to sink back from the door into the passage. She leaned against the wall, sick and trembling. Oh, dear Lord, how am I to bear this? Mother! Mother! Oh, my poor father! She could still hear their voices—terrible voices . . . "I'll have your blood for this, you cullion. . . ." "Alard, Alard, have pity. . . ." A foul name for her mother. "You have starved your dame; while you could think of nothing but iron and cinders . . ." that was Oxenbrigge speaking, Oxenbrigge the adulterer. . . . Catherine bared her teeth and her body shook with woe. She felt a hand touch her. "Come away, Mistress Catherine."

Robert Douce made her sit down in the hall and brought her a glass of wine. She was in too much of a stound to reject his services, though she wished him miles away . . . back in Robertsbridge—no, back in France . . . and better still if he had never come over. For some mad reason she felt that all this would never have happened had he stayed in his own country.

The voices in the parlour continued to rage, and then suddenly there was a clatter of swords and a long scream. Catherine and Douce both sprang to their feet. He told her to stand back, but did not wait to see what she did, and they both ran together to the parlour.

By the light of one dim candle, Alard and Oxenbrigge had crossed swords.

"Messieurs! Messieurs!" cried Douce. "Venez donc dans la salle. C'est impossible de vous battre ici! Impossible!"

It was the first time Catherine had ever seen him in any stress or agitation, and without knowing it he spoke his native tongue, which no one understood but Elisabeth Alard. The next moment he seemed to fall back into impassivity, standing in the doorway with his arms folded over his chest, watching the combatants as they lunged and parried. Squire Alard had put the candle on the table, whence his wife had snatched it up. She was holding it high on a wavering arm, so that shadows rushed over walls and ceiling, and seemed to join grotesquely in the battle, as if a dozen fiends fought in the dark instead of two English gentlemen.

Catherine cried:

"Let me go to my mother!"

But Robert Douce would not move from the door. It seemed as if her mother stood in the midst of a dreadful battle: shadows and swords all round her, flying and shuttling. She beat on Robert Douce's back to let her pass, but he would not move; he was like his own iron. Then for the first time she noticed the state of the fighters themselves, as they trampled about among the furniture, treading on lute strings. She saw that the Squire was winning, that he was pushing Oxenbrigge into a corner—she could hear the young man breathe hard, and suddenly she found herself wishing that her father would kill him.

At the same time she was aware of a commotion in the hall behind her, and turning round saw lights, and figures hurrying. The noise of the duel must have roused the servants, and here they all were, to witness the house's shame.

"Go! Go!" she cried. "Stand back!"

Then her mother's arm waved wildly, tossing the candle in the air; it fell extinguished, and for a moment there was complete darkness, a furious, noisy darkness, full of clashes and thuds—then the sound of a fall, the clatter of a sword rolling on the floor, and a deep groan. At that moment the lights came up, torches were brandished shakily, wavering across the ceiling, lighting odd corners of the room, and falling at last on the spot where Alard lay.

5

Robert Douce must have stood aside, for Catherine found herself kneeling by her father. Her fingers groped under his shirt, and came away blood-stained. He did not move; he did not seem to breathe.

She could not speak, but looked up at Oxenbrigge, as he stood, leaning against the window, his sword red half-way to the hilt. The servants were shouting and chattering but did not come into the room. Elisabeth Alard stood motionless with her arm stretched out and her hand lifted, as if she still held a candle.

"Mother," said Catherine. "Come and help me."

But she seemed unable to move; she could only stand there, holding her phantom light, and crying: "He's dead! he's dead!"

"Aye," said Catherine, her hand on her father's heart, "he's dead."

Then Oxenbrigge moved, crossing the room to the door.

"Stop him!" cried Catherine. "Stop him!"

But his bloody sword was still drawn, and no one cared to stand in his way.

"I killed the Squire in a fair fight," he said, turning at the door. "He bade me draw my sword and defend myself."

"But you killed him in the dark."

"He was pressing me hard, and I lunged. The darkness took us unawares."

Catherine could say no more, remembering how the darkness had come.

"I shall ride to my father's house," continued Oxenbrigge; "if any of the Squire's kin should seek me they know where to find me." And he marched out of the room.

"Oxenbrigge!" screamed Elisabeth Alard. "Oxenbrigge!"

But he was gone, his shameless footsteps ringing on the flagstones of the hall. Then a door slammed. . . .

She sank to the floor, a heap of crimson and purple silk. Catherine did not move—she could not touch her.

A woman came fighting her way through the servants, Margery Piers, her ladyship's own woman, stooping over her, patting her, soothing her, gathering her up from the floor and propping her with her arm.

"Come and rest, dear lady—come and rest. This hath been a sorry day for you. Come and rest."

She turned upon them all, as she led her sobbing mistress out.

"Poor soul! You should pity her—this is no fault of hers. 'Tis in her stars—her planets are combust."

6

It seemed a long time before the room was empty. Catherine stood looking at the floor, listening to the footsteps that tramped away, heavy and slow with the weight of her father's body—across the hall and up the big staircase to the bedroom where he would lie till the time came to carry him into Leasan churchyard. She knew that she should have gone with him, as her mother should have gone, to perform those last rites of washing and laying-out, which ought to be done by a man's kin.

But her heart was empty of filial piety, just as at the moment it was empty of grief and reprobation. Horror had swept it, and it was an empty chamber. Old Joan the nurse and housekeeper would see that her Master made a decent corpse —and she would not feel what Catherine would have felt when she looked upon his face.

"Father!" she cried suddenly. "Father!"

Her voice was automatic, and wrung with an anguish which was as yet only half conscious. Indeed, she hardly knew that she had cried out till a figure moved forward from the wall, and she saw Robert Douce.

"Is there anything I can do?"

She had forgotten all about him, and now she knew that he must have stood there the whole time, listening and watching.

"Is there anything I can do?" he repeated.

Her horror of him suddenly revived, and she cried angrily: "No—nothing more."

He did not seem to take her meaning.

"Had I not better go for a physician?"

She saw a chance of getting him out of the house.

"Aye—go—fetch a physician—go quickly."

"I shall ride to Hastings. The roads are dry for the season."

"Ride to hell if you choose!" and she ran from him to her room.

A clock struck ten. Had all this happened in an hour?

For the first time in her life Catherine could not sleep. She lay on her bed counting the hidden chimes as the hours danced slowly through the haunted night. Between three and four she heard movement and footsteps . . . that was no doubt the physician come to see her mother. But she would not rise. Madge Piers must care for her mother.

Her body felt weak and drained, but her head was like a lighted torch, blazing with cruel flames, as she rolled it to and fro upon the pillow. Twenty-four hours ago she had run away from the sorrows of Agnes Tuktone, but now she would gladly change places with her and her honourable wounds. . . . Conster had better have been burned like Fuggesbroke. Her father had better have died as a martyr than as a cuckold. Her mother had better have sat crazy on a stone than be lying in her bed weeping for her paramour.

Sometimes she blamed herself; she should have warned her father. Yet she had already blamed herself for letting such thoughts come into her head—she had called them wicked. She had told herself that life could not be as wicked as her thoughts. What would her father have said had she gone to him with such a tale? . . . But she should have gone to him. Oh, Father, Father! We've all betrayed you—your foes have been of your household. . . . Only Simon is guiltless—and what will he do? Soon he will be home again, and what will he find there?

Towards morning she must have fallen into a kind of sleep or daze of sorrow, for she opened her eyes to see daylight outside the window, with grey clouds and a slant of rain. She raised herself on her elbow, fully awake, yet with a troubled consciousness that someone was in the room. She could see no one, but the next moment there was a knock at the door.

"Come in."

Madge Piers came in.

"Oh, Mistress Catherine, her la'ship would see you presently."

"Why does my mother wish . . . I would say, how is she this morning?"

"Better, Mistress Catherine—much better since I made her

a betony pottage, with a pick of yarrow. Those are all herbs which answer the stars and keep the heavens smooth."

"But the physician—did he come?"

"Surelye, Mistress—came and took half a pint of blood from her. But that's no answer to the stars at all. What you mun find is their answering herbs on earth, which is a wisdom my mother taught me and much thought of in her day among scientists and physicians, though now they think of näun but blood——"

"Hold your tongue, Madge. I'll come and see my mother."

She rose and dressed hurriedly, eager to have this meeting over and done with, but in the disorder of her mind forgetting to fasten her gown. She tapped on her mother's door, afraid of what she might see.

"Is that Catherine? Come in."

The voice sounded unexpectedly brisk, and when Catherine entered the room she had a surprise. Instead of being in bed, her mother sat in a chair by her toilet table, wearing her blue samite gown, her Flanders lace ruff, with her hair dressed high in ringlets. Her face was pale, but that was nothing new since it had become fashionable to imitate the Queen with a pale complexion. The change from the distraught and di- shevelled woman of last night was almost as great a shock to Catherine as that woman herself had been.

"Mother," she faltered.

"Come here, Catherine. Don't stand and gape . . . Lord save us, child! Where have you been? What a state you're in! —your hair is all uncombed, and your gown's unfastened; fas- ten your gown."

Catherine fastened it, her face crimson, for she remembered her mother's unfastened gown last night. How could she now . . . but perhaps Elisabeth remembered too, for she turned away her head and spoke more uncertainly:

"Have you slept to-night?"

"Aye. I slept an hour."

"More than I have, I'll warrant. But you were ever a plough- boy."

Catherine's face darkened with a flush.

"Mother, you mustn't speak to me like that."

"And why not?"

"Not after last night."

94

"Catherine!"

Both their faces were crimson now as they faced each other.

"What hath last night done for us?" asked Elisabeth Alard, again speaking uncertainly. "Am I not your mother still?"

Catherine made no reply.

"Speak, Kate! Am I not your mother?"

Catherine burst into tears.

Elisabeth watched her silently for a moment, then turned her head away, covering her eyes.

"You would say you can't forgive me for loving any man besides your father. You're too thick and loutish to have seen all that I've suffered in the past year—how lonely I've been, with your father thinking of his building and his furnace before ever he thought of me . . . but I won't speak evil of the dead. I'll only say that I've been lonely, and all you did was to tear and trapse about the country, looking like Wild Joan, with never a thought in your head but recusancy. How many hours have you spent with your mother? You might have made me forget I was lonely, but you were never at home save to sleep and to snap off your meals. I tell you, you've had your guilt in this."

Catherine could not speak.

"And now you think to have done with me," continued her mother, "but I ask, what are you to do without me? Your father's money comes to me until your marriage, and I see no chance of that. Your Uncle Thomas Alard will take over this place and certainly turn us out of it, as he hath his own wife and family. I can't see how you are to live without me."

"Mother, I haven't done with you."

"But I'm your mother no longer."

"I never said it."

"You think it. You love me no more."

"Mother, how can I love you after last night?"

"If you'd ever loved me at all you'd love me still. I've told you how your father himself drove me into a kinder man's arms . . . and your own neglect. I've told you that you must answer for it."

"Aye, but it wasn't only that you loved my cousin. . . . Mother, you—you wished my father killed . . . you—you dropped the light. . . ."

Elisabeth's face darkened with rage.

"Silence, malkin! How dare you tell such lies? I dropped the light, forsooth! . . . I, shaking like an apse with fright and misery . . . hold your lying tongue or you will rue it."

Her eyes blazed and her little fists shook upon her lap.

"If you hadn't dropped the light my father would have stuck him."

"And that would have pleased you, doubtless, malkin. You'd have been pleased to see lie dead the loveliest man that ever walked alive."

"The dirtiest traitor."

"Is it treachery to take what another man wants so little that he leaves lying about?"

"You know my father loved you."

"Once . . . once, long ago. But let's talk no more of him. He lived and died a gentleman—I bear him no malice, and I hope he bears me none. I would tell you, Catherine—that's why I sent Madge for you—I would tell you that I shall pack up and leave this house before my brother comes, and you must be ready to leave with me."

"Whither?"

"My brother Burdett's house by Colchester. He hath a great place and we can stay there for a while."

"How long?"

"I can't say how long."

"Till you marry Oxenbrigge?"

"He is gone to Flanders. He sent me word that he is gone to Flanders."

She spoke cheerfully; indeed, it seemed to Catherine almost as if a smile were at the corners of her mouth.

"He will stay there," she continued, "until this affair is smoothed over. After all, it was a fight between gentlemen. But one can never tell what my brother Alard will do—he may make trouble, though he inherits a fine property. I will not meet him, Kate—I must not meet him. We will go as soon as your father is buried."

"I shan't come with you."

"Forsooth! And where will you go?"

"I know not—but nowhere with you. This hath fixed me."

"Will you stop here? I doubt if my brother will have you."

A certain sharp anxiety was in her voice, as if she feared to leave Catherine's tongue behind her.

"I reckon he won't, neither. Anyway, I shan't stay here."

"But where will you go?"

"I shall go to my brother."

"Your brother—to Simon?"

"Surelye. There's none other I can go to."

"He's in Italy—in Rome—across the sea. You can never go there."

"He sent me word that he is coming home."

Elisabeth Alard's face changed—it seemed to grow suddenly shrunken and afraid. Her voice shook as she asked:

"When is he coming?"

"I can't tell you—soon."

"Then I must be gone, and you must come with me. How can you say you will go to him? Where will you find him?"

Catherine opened her mouth to say "Chichester," but thought better of it.

"He will send me word."

"Will he, indeed? And what shall you do when you have found him? You can't go with him. He's one of the Queen's enemies, an outlaw with a price on his head. He'll never thank you for your company. He'll send you home again—and what will you do then?"

"Mother, don't plague me."

"I?—plague you? That's fine, that's fair! Surely no poor woman ever had such a plague of a daughter. Hard girl! I'd thought our sorrow might bring us together, but I see that you are too hard to be melted even by sorrow."

"Sorrow!" cried Catherine, and laughed loudly as she walked out of the room.

8

Outside the door, she met her mother's woman.

"So, Mistress!" cried Madge Piers. "You have made her cry again."

"I haven't made her cry—but she hath made me laugh. Ha! Ha! Ha!

> 'I mun be married a Sunday,
> I mun be married a Sunday,
> Whosoever shall come that way,
> I mun be married a Sunday'

Ha! Ha! Ha!"

"Oh, Mistress, for shame. How can you treat her so?"

"A-done, do, Madge, with such talk. My mother's no more crying than I am. Ha! Ha! Ha!

> 'I his lamb, and he my coney,
> I mun be married a Sunday.'"

Madge tossed her head and passed her, going into the room, from which a low sound of sobbing now came. Catherine's harsh mirth ceased in bewilderment. She could not understand her mother, who seemed to be two different people, both of whom were strangers.

Was it really in the power of the stars to work such changes? Could the movement of heavenly bodies thousands of miles away make a chaste woman wanton and a kind woman cruel? Religion said they could not, but science favoured the idea; and though it was true that physicians nowadays blamed the humours of the body rather than the stars for mortal ills, they still relied for remedy on the earthly pattern of heavenly things which the herbs make upon the field. Five years ago her mother had been a gentle, distant woman, a little vain and proud of her beauty and her wealth, and contemptuous of the rough ways of the Alards, but never unchaste, never unkind either to her husband or her daughter. Surely such a change in her must have come from without, from adverse signs, unfavourable aspects, combust stars and a corrupting of the meteoron. . . . Catherine's mind seemed to sink into a pit of mechanical horror, of a world moved soullessly from without, of a determined universe of stars and fate in which there was no room for God or grace or personality or freewill . . . the sickness of her mind suddenly became physical, and she reeled, staggering against the wall.

For a moment everything went black, and she thought she would faint—had fainted, for a thousand ages seemed to pass. Then suddenly she was once again in sunlight, leaning against the wall.

9

She turned into her bedroom, and began mechanically to arrange her gown and her hair. In a few moments there was a knock at the door, and in walked Nan Jordan.

"Pardee, Mistress Catherine! You look all amort. What hath come over you?"

"I'm well enough. So leave me."

"But what of your breakfast? I'll lay you've had nothing to eat this morning or last night."

"I've no stomach for eating."

But she'd no sooner said it than she knew that she was hungry.

"Let me fetch you a bite—just a snap here in your room. And some sack—that 'ud put a heart in you."

"Aye, then; fetch me some sack and pasty."

It was queer, but until Nan spoke she had not known that she was hungry. Now she knew that her belly ached—had been aching ever since she woke—with faintness and emptiness. It was now high morning, and she had not supped the night before. Small wonder she was hungry—small wonder she had felt sick.

"Run, child!" she cried.

"I fly, Mistress. You shall have it in the twinkling of a hobby-horse."

She ran off and was soon back again with half a pigeon pasty, some cheese, a salad, French bread, and a big jack of ale. She set out the meal on Catherine's clothes-chest, and the girl fell to and devoured it. As she ate, her spirit seemed to revive. It was as Nan had said—the food put a heart in her. Not only did she lose her giddiness and faintness, but also that giddiness of soul which had made her swoon in the midst of a nightmare universe—a universe which seemed now to recede and dwindle till it became a mere pomander ball dangling at the hand of God, His gift and ornament.

"Oh, God," she prayed as she ate, "forgive me for doubting Thee—let me never doubt again. Oh, God, forgive us all our sins which have spoiled Thy plans for us."

It was the first time she had prayed since she set out for Fuggesbroke two nights ago. In her horror and despair she had not prayed at all. She wanted pardon indeed. What would become of her if she ceased to pray?

She buried her head in the jug of ale and drank deeply.

Sicut cervus . . . she could remember her psalter—the thirsty stag panting for the streams. My tears have been my bread day and night, while they say to me: where is now thy God? *Judica me, Deus* . . . She and Simon had listened to those words many times in the darkness of Leasan Church.

Now she would most likely never hear them again. *Introibo ad altare Dei* . . . the Altar of God—God the gladdener of my youth. My youth is gone. *Spera in Deo* . . . I must remember my Latin. While my body feasts and my soul fasts I must remember my Latin in case I should ever need it again. There is still hope. *Spera in Deo*. Oh, God my firmament, arise and help us and give us back our holy things, for we go weak and silly without them, and act wrong. Reckon there's only a few of us who can live without our tokens.

Her meditation with her face in a jug of ale was over; the ale was finished, and she set down the jack and wiped her mouth. She felt refreshed both in body and soul. Her body was warm, glowing and tingling, and her soul felt strong and free. The sweet fumes of the ale clouded round her head like summer. She knew that hope was not lost. Fuggesbroke might lie in ruins, but it was only the casket that was broken —the treasure was still inviolate in the bound body of Francis Edwards and the pierced heart of Richard Tuktone, in the free, living heart of Simon Alard, now homeward bound with a new hoard of riches.

The thought of her brother filled her with hope and courage. He was on his way home; in a very short while he would be back in England, at her side in all the new power of his priesthood. He would finish the work that had been begun— he would comfort Tuktone and reconcile Harman. He would say Mass for them all at Fuggesbroke or Colespore or wherever they could meet together. With Simon at her side she saw herself still of some shape and usefulness in the world—and free, for she would be free now; all her ties were broken save those which bound her to him. Her mother had no claim on her after this—she was free to go where she chose. At present she could make no definite plans, but her head sang with a general sense of hope and independence. She sat scheming vaguely and gloriously while Nan brushed and pinned up her hair and put her into a clean gown.

"Master Nicholas Pecksall came here this morning."

"When? Why wasn't I told?"

"You were asleep, Mistress, and he would not have you roused. He came to see your mother."

"What said he to her?"

"I know not. But it was about his ma'ship's burial."

"I reckon he said more to her than that. I will ride over and see him when I'm dressed. But I will look at my father first."

She had not been near her father's body: she had not dared enter the room where he lay. But now she felt brave enough for that too, and saw her former avoidance of him as undutiful. She must go and give him a Christian prayer.

He was laid in one of the spare chambers, on the bed. She went in and found candles burning at his feet. Though the old funeral service was gone, the old customs remained; besides, who would dare leave a dead man in a room without candles burning? The sloping light of the forenoon came in through the big modern window he himself had built, and lay on the sheet that covered him. Catherine would not raise the sheet. She felt her heart swell and her throat tighten. She knelt down to pray . . .

"And while some piece of his soul is yet within,
Some part of his funerals let us here begin,
    He will go darkling to his grave.
Neque lux, neque crux, nisi solum clink,
Never gentleman so went toward heaven, I think."

She could not remember where the words came from, but they seemed to fit the moment. There lay her father, a gentleman, an apostate, a cuckold . . . the kindest father and the best heart that ever breathed. The tears oozed between her fingers as she knelt. Oh, Father, Father. . . . She thought of how he and she had danced a jig together at Oliver Harman's wedding. How merry and how lively he had been, not knowing the dishonour that already lived in his house. Oxenbrigge . . . her kneeling body shook with hate and shame, as her old thoughts rose like bats. It was dreadful to think that she once had nearly loved him, that she had dreamed of his black hair under her hand, of his arms about her and his kisses on her mouth. Even to have ignorantly dreamed these things seemed to shame her now, to make her feel as if she moved shrinking across the stage of some old incestuous play . . . great black hangings and tiny wicked figures strutting to the lascivious drawl of viols. . . . She shuddered: she must escape out of this nightmare; she would not think any more of her mother and Oxenbrigge. Her mother had enough guilt towards her father without that. How dared she say that he had stopped loving her? He had loved her as he had loved them all, in his rough, faithful way. Gervase must say a Mass for him . . . *Neque lux, neque crux*—he had died without the faith he had renounced, but maybe his sufferings had wiped out his sins . . . the sufferings of that short last hour of life . . . She must pray for his soul.

She said the *Dirige* and the *De Profundis*, then rose from her knees, and, without looking towards him, went out.

On the landing she found Robert Douce.

11

She had forgotten that he was in the house, and at the sight of him the peace that had come to her in her father's room ebbed away. With a recoil of disgust she remembered his part in last night's doings; he stood before her under the double rebuke of two nights—Tuktone's and Alard's. For a moment she scarcely knew which she hated him for most—his betrayal of Tuktone's hope or his witness of Alard's shame.

She did not speak, but he read her mood in her averted face.

"So, Mistress—I have displeased you?"

She made to pass him; then suddenly indignation got the better of her.

"Why are you still here? Have you stayed to make sport of us?"

He looked bewildered.

"I come from the furnace."

"The furnace? And have you been to Fuggesbroke? That made a valiant furnace. Why did you not go there to see your work?"

He still looked quite blank and uncomprehending.

"I do not understand."

For the first time she doubted what she had been so sure of. His great melancholy eyes stared at her in a kind of sorrowful wonder—there was no blink of uneasiness or self-righteous stare.

"I do not understand," he repeated.

"Would you tell me that you've had no hand in the burning of Fuggesbroke?"

"I? No—not I. What could I have had to do with that? I heard it had been burnt only when I went yesterday to the furnace. They told me there."

"But—but I can't—I can't believe . . . Who else 'ud have told about the Mass and had soldiers sent out?"

"I know nothing of any Mass."

"But your daughter—did she never tell you there was to be Mass? Tom Harman—" She caught herself in time. "I reckon your daughter's at the bottom of all this."

He smiled.

"Maria! But she is a bride. She thinks of nothing but her new husband and her new house. She troubles not her head about religion. And how should she know what is doing at Fuggesbroke? Think you she is a spy?"

Catherine found herself blushing.

"Aye—I thought, and all the Catholics around here think, that you both are spies—Huguenot spies."

For a moment Robert Douce seemed startled, then he recovered himself and smiled again his melancholy smile.

"They think that because I have suffered for my religion I should find comfort in making others suffer? No, Mistress Catherine. That may be so with some men, but it is not so with me. I would do nothing to make Papists suffer either in their bodies or in their estates—for the very reason that I myself have suffered in both. I have lost my health and my inheritance, my father's house and my father's love, my twin brother whom I left behind in Beauface, my wife, Maria's mother, who died of her miseries as we fled from our home. I have lost all the loves and hopes and promises of my life. And it is because I have suffered all this for my religion that I would never do anything to make any man suffer for his, no matter how false I hold his religion to be."

"Then I reckon folk 'ull never hold you a true Protestant."

He shrugged his shoulders.

"If they will not hold that, they will be fools. My afflictions bear witness for me without my needing the testimony of another man's."

Catherine still felt bewildered, and newly embarrassed.

"But—but—I can't understand . . . we all took you for a spy. The Tuktones were sure of it."

"The Tuktones of all people might have understood me.

103

But they were afraid, and I am a stranger. That explains it, perhaps."

"But who can have betrayed us if you didn't?"

"Who? Why, any one."

"But the thing was known only to our friends . . . I'll never believe that any one of our friends is a traitor. I wöan't—I can't believe it."

"Not a traitor, but perhaps a little talkative?"

"I wöan't believe——"

Then suddenly she felt herself beginning to tremble and she knew that she had turned pale. She wanted to put her fear into words, but it was mixed with anger and it choked her. Robert Douce was speaking.

"It might be well not to trouble yourself too much as to who it was, for in these matters there is a sort of common rumour, and it is often impossible to tell how news gets about. One has spoken, but doubtless many would have spoken if he had not. Besides, the affair is over—the harm is done, as you would say. Better not afflict yourself now by suspecting your friends."

"Or myself."

"Yourself? No, I spoke not of you."

"But if it was he, it was myself. If Pecksall . . . then it was because I told him. Mounseer Douce, you spoke of Nicholas Pecksall?"

"I have been told that Master Pecksall laid the information, but doubtless many tongues——"

She seemed to fall back from him through the open door behind her, and before he could finish his sentence it had crashed between them.

12

Alone in her bedroom, she held her head in her hands and tried to think.

Nicholas Pecksall . . . She might have guessed . . . But Robert Douce was lying—lying to save himself. No, there had been truth in his voice and in his eyes, and it would have been a sorry lie to tell her, for she could expose it in the next hour. He said he had been told of it; then there must be a common rumour, common knowledge, and this was the very thing Nicholas Pecksall would do out of his hatred of

Fuggesbroke . . . Yet the betrayal of Fuggesbroke was the betrayal of the Church, and Pecksall did not hate the Church; also, but for the difference of a few hours, it might have been the betrayal of Catherine herself, whom certainly he did not hate. She could not believe him capable of sending her to prison, perhaps to death. She remembered how desperately he had pleaded with her not to expose herself, not to run these risks—she had even despised him for his everlasting talk of safety.

After all, a common rumour might be wrong—was perhaps likely to be wrong. Folk would expect the parson of a parish to lodge information against any recusants within its boundaries. And though she had told him there was to be Mass at Fuggesbroke, she had not told him the day. How had he known the day? He could not have known it. Fuggesbroke must have been betrayed by someone else with better knowledge—Harman, perhaps. She did not like to think so black of him, but she found in her heart that she would rather think black of Harman than black of Pecksall.

For if Pecksall had betrayed them, it was her work. It was she who had told him there was to be Mass. She had been—what was it Robert Douce had said?—"a little talkative." But only because she did not believe him capable of doing such an evil thing. She still did not believe him capable of it. He might blow with the wind, he might conform for safety's sake, but that was very different from deliberate attack and betrayal. Pilate she would believe him, but never Judas . . . though Mary Tuktone had called him that . . . "Judas was kind—and kissed" . . .

Perhaps he had made some sudden discovery that he was under suspicion and had done this to clear himself with the Protestant powers . . . She could not think . . . That was why she must know. She must ride over to Leasan and confront him with her suspicions. He would not lie to her—no, not unless his whole being had suddenly been changed by some Satanic miracle . . . So many strange and terrible things had happened in the last two days that perhaps Satan was at large again, walking up and down the earth as he had walked in the days of Job. And now there was nothing in the land to scare him away—no Masses, nor prayers, nor holy water, nor sacred images—so that no wonder he was a free rover . . .

Oh, God my firmament . . . She tried to pray, as she had prayed over her ale and pasty, for her fear of the universe was returning in a new disguise; but she could not find comfort now in that way—she had better seek it in action, run to the stable and call for her horse, and be galloping Kate again, galloping over Starvencrow Hill.

13

It did not take her long to make herself ready, and in a few minutes she was off. Soon her uncertainty would be ended, and Robert Douce proved a liar, or Harman a traitor, or Pecksall . . . but she would not think. While she was in the saddle she found it possible not to think. The easy canter of her horse, going his accustomed way, the creak of leather, the thud of hoofs on the turf, brought a sort of lulling emptiness to her mind. The morning swept over her, the September morning, now full of new sunshine, of soft wind and scented decays. She saw herself cantering through it eternally, without past or future . . . an eternal present—eternal life . . . eternal motion—eternal rest.

Leasan spire roused her from her comfort. She rode up to the rectory; it looked so innocent—surely it could hide no dreadful secret of broken faith. The roses were overblown now, nodding their heavy heads together, and strewing their white and pink petals on the garden ways. As Catherine walked up among them, a scent came from them that was stronger and sweeter and sadder than their wont in summer-time. She could see Pecksall nowhere in the garden, and when she knocked at the house door, his housekeeper answered it and told her he was in church.

"He hath gone to read prayers. Will you wait till he comes back?"

"No—I will go and find him."

She could not wait, either in the house or in the garden. She must move. So she walked back through the roses, across the garden to the wicket gate that led into the churchyard. The church door stood open, and she went in; the next moment she wished that she had not.

The interior of Leasan Church always disturbed her—the whitewashed walls and the communion table that stood in the middle of the chancel like a shovel-board. She had never seen a church fully furnished in the Catholic way, but she was old enough to remember an altar under the east window, for Nicholas Pecksall had not moved his till strictly ordered, and even after the stone altar was gone a little wooden one had taken its place on those early mornings of long ago when she and Gervase and one or two others had gathered on Sundays for Mass.

A little thin bell began to toll in the steeple, and suddenly Catherine caught sight of Nicholas Pecksall, standing like a ghost, tall and white in a long surplice that flowed from his shoulders to his feet. He stood at the side of the chancel arch, and a great Book of Common Prayer lay open on the desk before him.

"'Enter not into judgment with thy servants, O Lord, for no flesh is righteous in thy sight."

His voice seemed to roll round the church. The bell stopped and the clerk came hurrying from the steeple, to take his stand opposite the Parson and answer the Prayers.

"Dearly Beloved Brethren, the Scripture moveth us in sundry places . . ."

Catherine stood motionless. She wondered if he could see her. She did not feel sure. The church was dim with coloured glass, and she stood in the shadows by the font. On the other hand, it seemed unlikely that she could stand there by the open door and not be seen. Yet if he saw her, would he read grandly and sonorously like that?

". . . to acknowledge and confess our manifold sins and wickedness, and that we should not dissemble nor cloke them before the face of Almighty God our heavenly father . . ."

The words were reaching her now and she felt the shock of the English language. Its use seemed to her hail-fellow and irreverent, though the English was not that of common speech, but the language of the court and universities. It was years now since she had heard him read from the new Prayer Book . . . No, not years, but last week at Maria Douce's wedding. But that seemed years ago . . . It was very different now—standing at the back of the empty church and watching him there in his tall ghostliness, speaking like a king to a king. As she stood and watched, she became in time most curiously impressed. There he stood, seeming half as tall again, with a shaft of the haggard light upon him, and his face lifted into it while the great solemn words came from him slowly like a royal proclamation.

"Wherefore I pray and beseech you as many as are here present, to accompany me with a pure heart, and humble voice, unto the throne of the heavenly grace, saying after me . . ."

With a crackle of starch and creak of oak the tall figure sank down and the spell was broken. Catherine slipped out of the church, wondering how she could have stayed in it so long.

14

She finished her waiting in a room filled with books—books lining the walls and piled upon the seats and strewn upon the table where lay his half-written sermon on the text: "My babes, let us not love in word, neither in tongue; but in deed and verity." She had time to study these things before he came, for it was twenty minutes before he bustled in, his cassock flapping round his heels instead of bunching at his waist as usual.

"Catherine—my dear child."

He took her hand, and for a moment she was discountenanced by the warmth of his welcome.

He continued: "I'm thankful you've come, for I shouldn't have had time to-day to ride over to see you. I was at Conster early this morning, but I would not have you wakened, knowing what sleep must mean to you."

"I—I mun see you," was all she could find to say.

"Will you take a glass of wine? I have some Portugal wine that would do you good."

She shook her head. His kindness hurt her more than any quarrel.

"Let me fetch it—it will put a heart in you."

"Thank you. But I've just eaten. I want nothing."

He saw that she was wretched, and would not press her further. He sat down opposite her, and took her hand as it lay upon the table.

"Kate, I wish that I could comfort you."

It was the first touch of human consolation that she had been given since all her misery began. For a moment her hand lay in his—a warm, dry, strong clasp, to which her fingers yielded, and which seemed in some strange way to reach and warm her heart . . . Then suddenly she remembered, and pulled back her hand.

He looked surprised, and she realized that he did not know why she had come to see him. He thought that she had come for comfort in the ruin of her home.

"Catherine," he said, "you know that I'm your friend?"

His words gave her an opportunity.

"I äun't sure—not for certain. That's why I've come."

"What mean you?"

He had coloured, and she wondered if it was with guilt or with affront. She forced herself to speak calmly.

"Will you tell me how the news got around that there was to be Mass at Fuggesbroke?"

"Such news never got around," he answered readily, "or the soldiers would have been there when Mass was said instead of seven hours earlier."

She saw that he was quibbling, and she knew now that ever since he had come into the room she had hoped as she had never hoped before that he would be able to prove his integrity. Her heart sank painfully. She wanted to lay her head upon the table and weep, but for some time longer, till she really knew for certain what she feared, she must go on struggling with words.

"Who sent them to Fuggesbroke?"

"How can I know?"

She said with difficulty:

"I believe it was your doing."

The colour spread over his face, and this time she felt sure it was a blush of guilt. For a few moments he did not speak, and while the silence hung heavy with the smell of books in the little, close room, she wondered if he would lie to her or for a time go on questioning and quibbling. At last he said:

"Why should you think so?"

"You're the only soul who knew of our plans save Thomas Harman, and I'll never believe that he's betrayed us."

"Why should you never believe? . . . But no, I won't argue unfaithfully. I'll face up to my own deeds, for I didn't act without my conscience."

"Then this was your doing."

"It was."

She half rose in her seat, then fell back. She could not speak.

"Catherine, don't mistake me."

She almost laughed.

"How am I to take you, then?"

"You mustn't think that I did this out of enmity towards the Pope or even towards the Tuktones. I did it all for your sake—to save you from the grievous fate you were bringing on yourself."

"But if I had been there . . ."

"I knew you would not be there at that time of night; which was one reason why I laid the information myself, fearing that if I left it to others the soldiers would find you at Mass. You would certainly have gone to prison for hearing Mass, and 'tis likely would have been made to share Tuktone's guilt of harbouring, for which the punishment is death."

"But why should I have been found at Mass? Who should find me if you had held your tongue?"

"You'd surely have been found; if not now, then at some other time. Mine isn't the only tongue in the parish that can speak."

"But you were the only one who knew of our plans."

He smiled wearily.

"By the time I spoke, your scheme was known—I won't say in particular, but at least in general—throughout the neighborhood."

"I'll never believe it."

"If you won't take my word I can prove nothing to you. I can only say that the report was general, and it seemed to me that the only way to save you was to act quickly and confine the mischief to Tuktone. Praise God that I succeeded."

"So you can praise God for that . . . dear God! . . . But I'll never believe our friends were talking, that they betrayed us. Make not such excuses for yourself, for I'll have none of 'em."

"I need no excuses. I did as seemed right to me. But in sober honesty, there was a report. Tuktone hath ever been suspect, and now I believe there hath been talk of Harman too. Have you never heard what your neighbourhood is called by folk in my parish?"

"No. What is it called?"

"Superstition Corner. That's how the folk in Leasan and in Vinehall begin to talk of the countryside round Holly Horns—Fuggesbroke, Conster, Holly Crouch—Superstition Corner."

"And what's the harm of it?"

"Much harm—since it shows that they smell the Pope. And in the last week they've talked plainly of a priest being expected at Fuggesbroke."

"They couldn't have known."

"They knew, and why shouldn't they know? The matter was spread over two parishes."

"Only among friends."

"Who doubtless talked of it to one another and maybe let fall a word or two before a maid or a farm-servant. Anyway, I tell you it was all about."

"So you made sure it should get to the right ears."

"I did. I went to the magistrates at Vinehall, at Pesenmarch and at Rye——"

"You went to Rye!"

"I thought I should get quicker action. Remember, I wanted that priest caught some hours before his Mass could begin."

Catherine rose to her feet, but found that she could not stand steadily. She was shaking from head to foot, and had to lean on the table for support.

"And how much did they give you—thirty pieces of silver?"

His colour deepened.

"You make too much of a to-do about this. I've told you that I didn't act out of enmity towards the Church, which is no better served by such as Tuktone than it is served by the King of Spain. My object was your welfare."

"So you used my confidence to betray my friends. You've made me their traitor. When I was at Fuggesbroke they as good as said it was my doing, and I denied it because I thought they meant the tale had come through Harman and Robert

Douce. I never thought . . . they never thought . . . I never thought it had come through you. I trusted you. I was a fool, but how was I to know you were my enemy?"

"Kate, I am not your enemy."

He too had risen, and came round the table to where she stood shaking and weeping.

"Kate, can't you understand? I've done this only for one reason—one only—only because I love you."

She gaped at him.

"Yes, I love you. I've loved you these ten years at least. When I saw you were in danger I had to stop your folly. And the only way I could stop it was to strike at your friends. So I told the magistrates that a priest would be at Fuggesbroke this Monday evening . . . I was in terror lest they should come for him too late and maybe find you there, so I told them that he would be there only a few hours, that he would be gone by midnight. It is no triumph to me that he is taken. All I care is that they didn't take you."

He had shocked her so much that she was calm and cold.

"And this is a tale to prove your love."

"It proves that I thought of you, and you only."

"You've served me well by making me a traitor."

"Don't talk so bitterly, child. If I've made you a traitor, it is an innocent one. No folk in their wits would blame you."

"Folk an't in their best wits when they see their homes burnt down and their dearest murdered. No one at Fuggesbroke will ever speak to me again."

"I'm glad of it. I'm glad if my work hath ended your friendship with Tuktone. While you went to them you were never safe."

"Safe!"

"Yes, safe. Oh, Kate, you can't think what prayers I've said for your safety."

He was standing close to her now, and once more she was conscious of a buried fire of youth within him. She also felt again the tenderness which had so stirred her heart when he first came into the room.

"My Kate," he continued in a lower voice, "you can't conceive what sometimes I've endured when you would be so mad. I've almost wept for fear of what might come to you. I've told you that I love you—know you not what that means?"

"Seemingly it means that you set out to break my heart."

Her voice was no longer angry, but flat and sad. He came nearer.

"No, it means that I would cherish and protect you. I would keep you here safe with me instead of galloping over the country full of dangerous plans. Now all your mad plans have come to the ground, and I'm glad of it, because it gives me a better hope."

"Hope?"

"That you will let me care for you. Kate, what friend have you now but me? Will you turn from your only friend?"

"I had friends enough before you did your harm."

"I speak not of Tuktone. I speak of your home. Ever since I heard what happened there my heart's been heavy for you. Your father and your mother . . . both lost, though differently. I shan't feign that you haven't lost your mother too."

"Why do you say all this?"

"Because, as I've told you, I grieve for you, dear Kate. What can you do? Have you thought of what you will do?"

"No—only that I shan't go with my mother."

"Where can you go, then? . . . Kate, come here. Let this be your home."

For a while she had suspected his drift, but would hardly let herself think she understood him. Surely he would not crown his infamy by such a proposal . . . But now he had said it. His hand was on her wrist, his face was close to hers—ten years seemed to have dropped from him. His eyes were burning, not with passion but with tenderness, a heat that had no flame and yet was seven times hotter than any fire. She could feel it melting her heart—just tenderness . . . She must save herself quickly. She wrenched her hand away.

"How dare you say so to me? How can you think for one moment that I would—that I—I——"

"I've told you I love you. Is it such an insult that I should speak of marriage?"

"You know I would never marry you."

"Not now—but in a little while. In time you will come to see that I've done you a service rather than an injury."

"I shall never see it—never. And now I mun go. I won't stay here to be affronted."

She moved towards the door, but he slipped round the other side of the table and reached it first.

"Leave me not, Kate—leave me not like this. Stay and listen to me, if but for a moment."

She repeated sullenly:

"Let me go. I won't stay here to be affronted."

"Cease from that word. There's no affront in an offer of marriage."

"There is—from you. You know that you can't marry me. You know that however many times the Common Prayer was read over us we should still be a priest and his concubine."

He was angry now.

"How dare you say such an abominable thing? It is a lie. I can marry the same as any other man. Most men in my position would have married years ago—aye, even before the new religion came in. But I would not, because I loved you—I was attending you. Kate, Kate, can you not understand me a little?"

"No, I can't."

"But you must try. I can't bear to think of you alone in the world and hating the only friend who can help you. I can't bear to think . . . Oh, my child, I shouldn't have spoken now if it were not for all that's happened in your home. I know you must be angry with me for a while, even though you know it was all done for love of you. But I can't see you left worse than an orphan . . . I must save you and take care of you in spite of yourself."

"If I married you," she said, "I should lose the only comfort I have left in all the world—my religion."

"If you mean the Catholic religion, you lost that long ago."

"No, no, I have it still."

"You have not. You lost it long ago. The Catholic religion is lost for ever to this land. You must believe me."

"Then why did you teach me to love it?"

"Because I thought it would come back. But I was wrong, and now I would set that wrong right—the wrong I did you. The Pope's religion is gone beyond recall—I know that it will never come back. Its own friends have been its destruction. But no matter . . . why should it matter to us? There are other things in life besides the Catholic religion—even other religions. At least we have a sober, reasonable, learned remnant of religion left, and our future is with that. Besides, there are other things . . . there are books and there are roses, and there's love. We can be happy, Kate, without the Pope. We can be happy here, with each other and our garden and our books. I believe not that you've ever known what true happiness is, but I can teach you, if only you'll allow me—honey Kate, golden Kate . . . for the sake of the God who made more than one way to heaven, forget all these wild dreams which are nothing but vain hope and vain glory, and let me cherish and comfort you. I tell you that the Pope's religion is dead, but you're alive, Kate, and so am I——"

"Stop! Stop!" she cried, able at last to interrupt the stream of words that had flowed over her powerless mind. "Waste not your breath talking blasphemies. If you think your talk will change me, you're mistaken. I've suffered some tur'ble things in these last days, but I still have my immortal soul, and I an't going to have you make me lose it."

"But, Kate, what will happen to your soul if you're tossed loose in a Protestant world without kith or kind?"

"I shall have my brother—I shall go to my brother."

He looked surprised.

"To Simon?"

"Surelye. Simon is on—he will soon be back in England. I shall go to him and he will protect me."

"Foolish child! How can he protect you? His life is forfeit from the moment he sets foot on English ground."

But he could not rob her of the courage that the thought of her brother had given her.

"Then we can die together. I'd sooner die with a good priest than live with a bad 'un."

He gazed at her angrily and lovingly.

"You are curst."

"Aye, curst with false friends, but blest with true religion."

She suddenly pushed past him as he stood, and the next moment she had the door open.

"Kate, stay!—do not go."

He tried to take hold of her, but she was gone.

His arms swung back empty to his sides. He had never known what it was to hold her in them. Perhaps his love should have been bolder, readier to seize and clasp. But he had been afraid to woo her while her mind was set so far from his, and now, having for years been too slow, he had moved too fast, acted headily and scared her from him. He would not go after her now. He heard her running down the garden, and very soon he heard her horse's hoofs in the lane. But she would come back. He told himself that she would come back, as she had always come after their quarrels.

The sound of hoofs died away, and with a sigh he turned to his books. A new book lay on the table, substantial and inviting. He picked it up and settled himself in his chair. There are books and there are roses . . . and there is love, but love is no longer the greatest of these. It will help a man forget the pangs of a lost religion, but then in its turn it too has to be forgotten. Roses and books are better. Roses die and come again and their death smells as sweet as their life. Books are always under our hand, and can be opened and closed and thrown aside at will. They are bound but we are free . . . a tolerable conceit. There are books and there are roses, and there is good ale . . . he would send for some ale in a moment—ale and crusty bread and goat's milk cheese and some of his own good apples. The morning was nearly past and he was hungry. He had been late with his morning prayers . . . No matter; there is no canonical hour for them as there is for Mass, nor need they be said on an empty stomach. It was a needless labour to say them betimes, as some men did still. Roses and books and good ale . . . and maybe love when Kate comes back, but we will not think now any more of love for at the moment it is nearly as painful as religion.

Thus he mused, turning over the new, clean pages of the Reverend Richard Hooker's "Laws of Ecclesiastical Polity."

Chapter Seven

"I WILL go to Chichester," said Catherine.

She was riding up the lane between Leasan and Holly Horns, and suddenly the idea came into her head:

I will go to Chichester.

It had come to her with all the suddenness of an inspiration; it also yielded to reflection, after the manner of good inspirations, for the more she pondered it, the more it seemed a thing to do.

At Chichester she would find Father Edwards. He would be in the prison, most likely with Father Oven, the priest who had ministered at Fuggesbroke last year, and possibly with others who had not been afraid to venture for their faith. In the prison at Chichester she could still find honest men, who had not lost their integrity, who were prepared to die rather than compromise with truth, who would not offer her comfort and tenderness on a fork heated in the hell fire of apostasy, nor yet turn against her because others had made her a traitor, nor sell their honour for a false jewel called love.

At Chichester, too, she could wait for news of Simon. The Catholics there would hear of his arrival, and she would be able to see him directly he landed and stop his going to Conster, or at least prepare him for what he would find there. She now saw clearly that if she was to meet her brother she must go after him, or she would be swept away with her mother into Essex, into a Protestant household where he could never come to her.

If she went to Chichester she escaped her mother, who would be far too much afraid of meeting her husband's brother to waste any time in searching or waiting. The distances of life were still unprospected, but she felt that she would get a better view of them from Chichester than she could from Conster.

Instead of riding straight home she went round by way of Vinehall, and entered a little wood behind Lordaine Court. Here she tethered her horse to a tree and stretched herself in the shade. She wanted to think, and she would think best lying still, and she would think best away from Conster, because there she would think only of the past, and she wanted to forget the past and think of the future.

The future was all that mattered; the past was dead and black, even that past of scarcely an hour ago in Leasan. She must not let her mind dwell on it—she must forget. Lord help us all to forget . . . *Levavi oculos meos in montes*—no, no more Latin, for it was he who taught it to me.

She forced herself to think of the future, lying there in the wood, with freckles of sunlight upon her, and in her nostrils a sweet smell of earth and leaves and hop-bine. There was a field of hops just outside the wood, and now among them the pickers were at work—the voices of the men and women came to her softly on the wind and murmured among the leaves.

Up till this hour she had made no plans for her future, but now she saw clearly that she must plan at least for the next few days, or she would lose her freedom. She must leave Conster immediately, before there was any chance of her mother setting out. She must be up early to-morrow morning and off before anyone was astir. It would not take her long to ride to Chichester—probably no more than a couple of days. She could stay quietly in the town, and maybe she could go to the prison and visit Father Edwards and Father Oven . . . If she arrived in time only to see honest men strung up on the gallows she would see a better sight than she had seen for many a long, sad day.

Chichester had suddenly appeared as the sunny land of Goshen to her dark Egypt. Oh, it was true, just about true, what she had said to Pecksall—she had nothing left in life but her religion. Love was a false diamond and friendship a bunch of thorns, and a great wind from the desert had blown upon the four walls of her house. She could be happy only among those who, too, had lost everything but their religion—Francis Edwards and John Oven and one day Simon Alard, whom she would find at Chichester with other honest men.

Planning had become a kind of dreaming. Catherine had always despised hops as a foreign weed which made good ale taste bitter of Protestantism and the Netherlands; but to-day they brought her weary mind the boon of sleep. She breathed in their fragrance and her head grew heavy. It sank upon her arm, and she slept. For long hours past and future were wiped out in dreamless sleep, while round her the woods darkened into a green twilight. When she woke the sun was gone, and the voices of the hop-pickers were still, and Ball her horse was pawing the fallen leaves, knowing that the chills and terrors of darkness were rising up around him.

2

It was late when she reached Conster, the cockshut time when shadows are lost in the darkness which is not yet night. The place had a blind, deserted air, standing beside the river with unlighted windows and empty lawns. Riding up under the walls, she felt it loom above her like a fortress—Castle Shamefast . . . Suppose she should wake in the night and hear weeping—or a lute . . . She shuddered. She was glad that she was to spend only one more night there, and probably that night she would not sleep at all.

She took her horse to the stable and slipped into the house. There were voices and lights in the kitchen, but no servants were about; they had shut themselves in their own quarters to be as gay as they could. There was no sign of supper laid anywhere—doubtless her mother's had been taken up to her, and she would get her own from the livery cupboard and take it to her room. She found bread and pasty and some marchpane, but no ale. She would have to fetch that herself from the buttery. The house felt ghostly and empty, in spite of the servants squealing in the kitchen—no lights had been put anywhere, it was as if they feared to come out.

At last she was in her room. She set her meal aside; that would come later—at present she must think and plan. The first thing she did was to count her money—four golden angels and eight pistolets. That would take her to Chichester and further . . . should she ever get further . . . she mustn't think of it now. Her business was to get to Chichester, so that she could renew her trust in God and man. When she had met Simon she could plan further. At present she must be thankful to find she had so much money.

She considered what clothes she should wear, and a new thought came to her. Turning over the clothes in her chest, she found some of her brother's which for one reason or another had been stored there since his departure. It struck her then that she would find it better and safer to ride in man's clothes. Though generally regardless of her mother's warnings, she knew that there were dangers on the road. She had roamed about her own neighbourhood without much fear of rape or robbery, but she realized that things would be very different once she got beyond the country of Holly Horns. The roads, especially the great pack roads, swarmed with beggars, pikers and Abraham men, whose increasing numbers had been a problem to the magistrates ever since the Dissolution. A woman riding alone would be fair game for these pests, whereas they would think twice before attacking a man. After all, she had reasonably a man's figure; deficiencies of breast and hip which had sometimes been a distress and humiliation would be an advantage now. On horseback she could certainly pass for a man, and if she carried food with her she need not stop to eat at inns.

She examined her brother's clothes. They were in good condition and would doubtless fit her well, as he and she had always been of the same height and size. She tried on various garments, lighting every candle so that she could see herself in the long glass that swung between posts at the front of her bed. The clothes were, like her own, of an earlier make than was now the fashion, but such as were more generally worn in country districts than the new style. She finally chose a tawny woollen doublet, with flashings over a linen shirt, and a tight linen collar at the throat; breeches of russet kersey and cloth netherstocks, and a cloak of tawny cloth. There was only one hat, though that luckily a plain one, and her brother had left no shoes; but her own would serve, being of coarse, country make, without heels, and her feet had always been large enough for a man's.

She surveyed herself in the glass with some pleasure, and in her limbs was a delicious sense of freedom—it seemed delightful and strange to be no longer kicking at the folds of a great skirt. But she could see that something was wrong, and the next minute she realized that it was her hair, which was still as Nan Jordan had knotted it up. She then saw that she would have to cut her hair—there was nothing for it, and she did not care about it much. She had no need of beauty now.

In the room was a pair of sewing-shears, and with these she cut off her hair. She could not make a very good job of it—she could not give herself the sleek shining head of the modern gallant—but she could make herself look quite a good sort of country boy, and after all that was what she wanted. With the shearing off of her hair her sense of freedom seemed to increase and to take on a new quality. With her hair she seemed to lose something of her femalehood, of her woman's bondage, as if with her shears she cut off her sufferings as a woman and became a boy—one of those boys in a play, who only act a woman's part, and dressed in Cynthia's or Bethsabe's robes, seem to be neither man nor woman, but a free being. She turned on her heel, waved her hat and whistled a little tune. For long she had not felt so gay.

The gaiety passed, but still she felt free. Lighting a small fire in the grate, she burned the locks of her hair. She wondered if she should leave a word for her mother as to where she had gone, and finally wrote out:

"I have gonne to seeke my brother. Tarry not for me as I shall nevere come backe."

It was now scarcely past midnight, but she decided that she would not wait for dawn before setting out. She could not rest, and the first part of her journey was through familiar country, so could well be undertaken in the dark. Her horse needed only a few hours in the stable, having done no more yesterday than take her to Leasan. She had better be off before there was any chance of the household stirring. In another hour she would start.

She ate her livery, and on her way out helped herself to some more from the cupboard. With this and a feed of oats she meant to fill her saddlebags, taking no other luggage. She would not be worth robbing, but she must go armed: it would be folly otherwise. Her father's dag hung on the wall of the *privée*, but she did not take it, having no experience of firearms, which she regarded as dangerous and unprovidential. An honest knife would do for her best, and she took one from the armoury in her father's room, a French poignard in a sheath. She felt well protected.

If a year, or even six months ago anyone had told her that she would ride away from Conster without sorrow, she would not have believed it. But now she found that she had no grief at all. All that had made her love her home was gone or was doomed. Her father was gone, and in a manner of speaking he had been Conster, the spirit and hope of the house he had rebuilt. Without him the place seemed dead—even if her mother had not dishonoured it, she could not have kept it alive. And now strangers would come to it and it would be their home, and she and her father would be the ghosts of the place, mere memories hanging invisible.

As for the country itself, over which she had walked and ridden for so many years, she had no regrets for that either. Apart from all that she herself had suffered in it, she knew that it would change—change more terribly than the house. It would have changed, of course, if her father had lived, but for his sake she could have borne it. She could not bear it now. Her uncle would most certainly go on with the plans her father had made for developing the land. When he knew that there was iron in it, Thomas Alard would bid Robert Douce finish building his furnace, and in a few years' time all this land of Medyrsham and Wogenmarye would have become a hideous cinder-hill, its forests doomed to keep alight its forges, flames belching day and night and hammers thudding like ordnance.

3

The first part of her journey confirmed these thoughts. As soon as she had ridden beyond the country of Holly Horns, the day broke and she found herself in the neighbourhood of Battle and Ashburnham, on the borders of the iron country. Thence-forward it was a ride from furnace to furnace. At Penhurst, Brikeling, Dallington, Heyfield, furnaces were either blowing or in process of being set up. In the early dawn the flames of Penhurst and Ashburnham roared up and swept the Plough out of the sky. . . .

"Loud dub a dub tabering with frapping rip rap of Ætna" . . .

The road ran close to Penhurst forge and she could see the glare within and hear the thud and clink of the hammers, while men who looked like black devils danced to and fro in the light. So terrible did it all look that she made the sign of the Cross as she passed it.

By the time she came to Heyfield it was broad daylight, and the flames were to be seen only in the caverns of the forges. A cool, pale Michaelmas day lit up huge piles of cinders and clinkers, and hills of waste that still smoked dully, and little slab-castles that were being built to house the workers which the Squires were bringing from foreign parts both in England and France. The country was being destroyed —eaten up by the love of money expressed in fire and waste. Near the furnaces woodmen were at work cutting down the forests to feed them.

For almost the whole of her journey Catherine knew that

she would have to ride through this black country. Between the iron villages were great forests, with here and there a clearing for a farm. But the road, though shadowed and dark, was not lonely, for it was the high road to the West, and all along it went post-horses, pack-horses and wagons, carrying travellers and goods out of Kent into Hampshire, with by-roads down to the ports at Brighthelmsted, Hulkesmouth and Littlehampton. Among these travelled less importantly the population of the farms, flocks of sheep and geese, and hogs, being driven to pasture or to market. So far the road seemed pleasantly free from beggars, though there would be always two or three of them lurking on the outskirts of the villages, and on the village greens she often saw beggars in the stocks.

In the cool damp morning she was able to press forward as far as Buckstead. She had travelled comfortably and safely, and no one had spoken to her except to give the common greetings of the road. At Buckstead she found market-day and a strolling company of players doing "Mother Bombie" before the inn. The street was shadowed by the cool beech trees, and Catherine decided to bait her horse and sit down outside the inn, with a jack of ale to watch the players. She was glad to rest, and seeing that everyone was busy either with the market or the play, she hoped to be let alone.

A young girl, probably the innkeeper's daughter, came and brought her a dish of mirobolans. She seemed inclined to talk and ask questions. She asked if she had ever seen such a play —if she had ever seen "King David" or "The Woman in the Moon"—if she came from far and where she was going. All the time she looked at the bench on which Catherine sat, her bright eyes asking her to move along so that she could sit down beside her; but Catherine would not budge and answered only gruffly, with downcast eyes, so that in the end the girl went off, talking of louts and hoddy-doddies. Soon afterwards the players finished their play, picked up the tail of their cart and set out for the next village.

Their place, though not their audience, was taken by a wandering gospeller, a wild-looking man who spoke in the uncouth dialect of some foreign shire. Catherine understood enough to know that he preached Protestantism of a fanatical, anabaptist sort, demanding that the clergy should be driven out of their parishes, as they were but the old priests come back under another name, and that only grown folk should be baptized and that any man who felt the call of God should be a Minister without need of ordination. There was much of the "wicked and impious mysteries of the Mass," "the Scarlet Woman" and "Old Pope Antichrist," so that Catherine had some difficulty in keeping her seat. But she knew that she must not betray any Romanish sympathies, so sat there eating her mirobolans with a wry face, till in the end the market crowd decided that they too did not like the preacher, and carried him off with much laughing and whooping to throw him in the duck-pond.

When that had happened, she felt that she could safely pay her reckoning and go. She was glad to find that her manhood passed in a crowd and in such chance encounters as her journey led to. Ball, her horse, was refreshed after a two hours' bait and took her that day as far as Cookfield. Here she must spend the night. Before she left Conster she had planned vaguely to sleep out of doors, but now she saw that it would not do. Her horse must have proper stable refreshment if he was to carry her as far as Chichester tomorrow, and as for herself it might be dangerous to sleep out, as there were some queer characters on the road, especially at night. Crossing Ashdown Forest, she had passed a huge encampment of pikers and beggars, covering the hillside with their tents and litter, their dogs and nags and brats: she had been glad to tack herself on to the tail of a gentleman travelling with his servants and family to Billingshurst.

At the inn she had some difficulty in getting a room to herself, since she travelled alone, without baggage or servants. But as she insisted and offered to pay gold she was at last given a small attic with a very mean bed in it. She had taken the precaution of supping on the road with the food she had brought, for she was afraid to mix with the company at the inn table—she felt that if she spoke much she might betray herself, and was doubtful of her power to mix as a man with men.

But when she woke the next day, rested and refreshed, she found that much of this fear was gone. She was growing used to herself in breeches, and had therefore come to think that she could not be so very remarkable to others. It was simple enough for a woman of her make to pass for a young shy country boy, and while she drank her ale before setting out on her journey she had quite an easy conversation with a middle-aged man who started on the weather and then told her he had come east from Devon to learn the iron trade, being persuaded that the future wealth of England lay in iron rather than in corn.

Catherine was sorry for it, but inclined to believe him. All that night, under her sleep, she had heard the bumping of the hammers—boom, boom, boom, boom, so hard pressed that they must work by night as well as by day; while for the first part of the day her road led from furnace to furnace—Slogham, Bolneye, Shipley, Pulborough, all thudding and roaring, making ordnance of war, and railings and gates and andirons for the new nobility.

She was glad when at Pulborough she found herself on the Stane Street, riding southward away from the forest land, into the downs where there are no woods to burn. She was glad to leave it all behind her, this country of hammer and waste, which was spreading its plague into the country that she knew, to eat it up. She would be still more glad when she came to Chichester. Ball, her horse, was tired, and so was she, for she had not time to bait for more than an hour at Pulborough. But she did not want to spend another night upon the road, for though her journey had been made with an ease and safety she had not expected, she would be glad to reach its end. Besides, she did not know what time she had. The law sometimes moved swiftly against recusants—and her brother's ship might even now be in port.

Through Waltham, Bignore, Halfnakede . . . and she was riding into Chichester, under the Gate. Above the gate she saw heads stuck up on poles, and for a minute she was afraid that her friends might have already met their doom. But looking more intently she saw that the heads were rotten and must have been there some time, and the next moment her sense of smell confirmed her eyesight with a fine stink.

4

She decided to go at once to an inn, for she and her horse were both tired out; also at an inn she would hear the news of the town. She found the Saracen's Head in the market-place, and bespoke a room. She had eaten the last of the food

125

she had brought from Conster, so she would have to sit down to supper with everyone else; but by this time she had lost all her fears and knew besides that she must talk if she was to hear news.

There was a large company at table—farmers, merchants, a few parsons and their wives visiting the Cathedral, and one or two travellers on their way to the harbour. The number was too large for general conversation, and Catherine found herself next to a young man who told her that he had been waiting in the town some days for the arrival of his father, a merchant on his way from Lyons with gloves and silk.

"I look for him each day as it comes, but the winds have been unfavourable. They may have had to run along the coast."

"And how do you find the town?"

"Not so bad for what it is; but I come from London. Where do you come from, sir?"

"I come from Rochester in Kent and am on my way to Portsmouth. Howsumdever, I shall stop a day or two here and see the place."

"There an't much to see—only the Cathedral, and since you come from Rochester it won't be the wonder to you it is to some folk. I've heard some fine things of Rochester Cathedral."

Catherine had no wish to talk of Rochester Cathedral.

"Tell me," she said: "whose are those heads over the city gate?"

"I know not—I have not heard. I take it they've been there for some time. Maybe you, Sir," addressing a short man who sat ladling pease pottage down his throat across the table, "can tell us whose heads those are above the city gate."

"Mack, and I can, Sir! They're sheepstealers. I came into the city only yesterday, but I happened to ask the very same question that you've asked me, and I was told that they're two sheepstealers who were hanged at the Broyle a fortnight ago."

"You gentlemen talking of hanging?" asked the host, as he came down the table with the ale. "If any of you's in a mind to see a hanging, there's one to-morrow, and a fine one too— three seminary priests all to be hanged, drawn and quartered at the Broyle at nine o'clock."

Catherine put up her hands to her face, to hide the flush she could feel there. Luckily all eyes were upon the landlord.

"I shall go myself," he said, "and see the end of 'em—and so end all the Queen's enemies, I say."

"Amen," said one of the clergy, "but I would not go to see them hanged for all that."

"Then you will miss a fine sight, Sir. 'Tis long since we've had a proper noble hanging with speeches and prayers. Those thieves and beggars can do naught but groan and shiver till they're turned off. I went this last time and was mightily disappointed."

"Said you they were all priests?" asked Catherine in a voice she tried to make careless.

"All priests, my lad, and two of 'em have been in gaol a twelvemonth—those two that were taken at Littlehampton last Michaelmas. The third is only just taken, I hear, and there was a fourth besides, but when he heard his sentence he couldn't face it, so took the oath and abjured his treason. My son was at the trial and brought me a very pretty account of all that happened."

Catherine dared not speak. She sat there swallowing her pottage, and hoping that someone else would ask the questions that burned her tongue.

A man spoke from farther down the table, a clerkly looking person.

"I understand there was a Romish priest of the name of Edwards taken a few days ago in the country over by Rye. Is it he who is to hang?"

"The very same—Francis Edwards, a seminary priest from Rome."

"They've been sharp with his trial."

"'At, that they have. But there's been a warrant out against him since the Grand Armada sailed; and maybe they thought it well three priests should hang together."

"Maybe they were scared that if they didn't hang him quick he'd cheat 'em by dying of the plague. I hear the plague's in Chichester gaol."

"The plague!" cried a parson's wife.

"No, no, madam!" cried the landlord, "there's no plague in the gaol or anywhere else in Chichester. 'Tis only the sweat —you may take my word that 'tis only the sweat."

"The physicians have not decided," said the clerkly person; "it may be the plague, or it may be the sweat, or the spotted-fever."

"You seem mightily well-informed, Sir," said the landlord angrily.

"My brother is clerk to Mr. Lewkenor, one of the justices, so I have it from him."

"I warrant Mr. Lewkenor never said the plague was in Chichester."

"The physicians have not decided, but if it is not the plague it is a highly putrid sort of fever."

"There's always fever in the gaol, and I'll wager this is but the common sort. Anyway there an't no plague in Chichester, nor hath been this hundred year."

"That's hard to believe of a seaport town."

The conversation had now turned into a lively argument on the plague and other diseases from which the landlord declared that his city was free, while others recorded with relish instances they knew of plague, sweating sickness, spotted-fever, gaol-fever and Italian sickness, which they swore were all to be found at the harbour if not in the town itself. Catherine did not listen. She found it hard to swallow her food, though her object was to leave a clean plate so that none should know how deeply she was troubled.

So Father Francis Edwards was to die to-morrow . . . a vision of his pale, haggard face rose before her, with the small ridiculous objects on his pedlar's tray. . . . And Father Oven . . . was he one of the priests who were to be hanged, or was he the priest who had renounced his faith?—the two who were to be hanged were taken at Littlehampton—she was nearly sure she had heard the landlord say that—whereas Father Oven had been taken at Battle. . . . He must be the one who had apostatized. . . . If she could only know—yet what did it matter? Three were called and two were chosen: it didn't matter which two; and one apostate is as bad as another, whether he come from Battle or from Littlehampton —or from Leasan . . . but she had not ridden all this way to find another runagate. . . .

She was very tired, and when she had with difficulty finished her supper she went up to her room.

She was so weary that she managed to sleep a little, in spite of her agitation and in spite of the lice with which the bed was infested. But her sleep was more like a long, twisted, troubled journey than any peaceful rest. Faces moved before her—a pale face, with starting, anxious eyes above a pedlar's tray, the wooden yet distraught face of Mary Tuktone, her mother's face, flushed and grimaced with weeping, the crowned and grinning faces of the players at Buckstead, faces at supper, shovelling pease pottage into gaping mouths. . . . She was on horseback, riding, riding, riding, and before her rode an army, with heads on the ends of their lances. . . . A gallows reared up before her and corpses swung. . . . Nicholas Pecksall showed her his plague spot . . . a priest had *"miserere mei"* written on his girdle . . . and she was riding, riding, riding.

When she woke she felt heavy and unrefreshed. She had taken up some French bread for her breakfast, but she could not eat it. She would start out at once and see the hanging. She asked the chambermaid if she knew the names of the priests who were to be hanged, but the girl could tell her nothing save that they were all three Romish priests who had wanted to poison the Queen. Catherine did not trouble with her, but went down, paid her reckoning—since she would not sleep again in such a bed—and fetched her horse from the stable. It was barely seven o'clock, but already the streets were full of crowds on their way to the Broyle.

When they came to the city gate she found the way so crowded that it took her nearly ten minutes to ride under it. All round her people were fighting and struggling. It was market-day, and the country people were coming into the town with their produce; a number stayed at the Broyle, and some turned back from the gate, despairing of going in, but others would force their way through the crowd so as to get the best stands at the market while their neighbours watched the hanging—or possibly some were still Catholics at heart and did not want to see good men come to such an end.

A young man in the crowd told Catherine that there were still many Papists round about Chichester, mostly of the poorer sort.

"Old folk who can't forget the friars, or else such joltheads they can't change their minds; and I've heard tell of folk living in the Downs who don't even know the Romish religion's gone, though I can scarce believe it."

The spirit of the crowd seemed largely anti-Catholic, and Catherine had to be careful of her manners. She found it hard to listen quietly to some of the things that were said, not only against the priests, but against Richard Tuktone. People had heard of his death at the sack of Fuggesbroke, and it was said that there had been a plot to poison the Queen, and that he as well as the priests had been concerned in it. It was also said that he and Francis Edwards had been plotting such things together when the soldiers came to Rye—Hastings —Brighthelmsted—it mattered little so long as it was by the coast, for Richard Tuktone was declared also to have put guiding lights for the Spanish fleet when it came up the Channel in July, and in his coffers had actually been found letters from the Duke of Medina Sidonia.

Among much that was painful for her to hear, Catherine learned that the names of the other two priests were Ralph Crockett and Edward James, so she now knew for certain that Father Oven had refused his martyr's crown. The number of her honest men was dwindling . . . *miserere mei*. But one honest man would have been enough to save Sodom, and here were three—one for Chichester, one for Conster and one for Leasan . . . one for her father, one for her mother, and one for Nicholas Pecksall. . . . She felt strangely moved and exalted, almost light-headed, as at last she jostled her way under the gate and came out on the high-road leading to the Broyle.

About a mile farther on the gallows rose up before her, and she felt a curious fear and constriction of her heart. This would not be the first hanging she had seen, but it would indeed, as the landlord had said, be different from the others. To-day she would see men die, but not for their own sins. No doubt their sufferings would be a passion offered for the sins of the unfaithful—for the unfaithful that they did not know as well as for the unfaithful that they knew. These three friends would die expiating her father's conformity, her mother's adultery, her friend's apostasy: they would wipe her world clean as they left it. . . . Yet before they died she

130

would have to witness dreadful things, and for a moment her
heart failed her. Though she had never been squeamish, she
was glad to be on the outskirts of the crowd that swarmed
round the scaffold.

The day was warmer and sunnier than many that had gone
before it. There was no wind, and a haze hung over the
Broyle heath. Away across the meadows the spire of Chichester
Cathedral shone dimly in the soft light. It was all very peaceful, and, closing her eyes, Catherine could for a moment
imagine that the murmur of the crowd was a murmur of bees.

She was right on the edge of it, and behind her was a little
wood of sallows and alders, sloping down to the water-meads.
Backing her horse under the trees, she could feel the welcome
shade of them upon her head. She closed her eyes again and
prayed a little. Oh, that she could pray more . . . perhaps
when the martyrs died their sufferings would release her soul
for prayer.

Then suddenly a roar went up: "They come!"

She craned to see, and over the heads of the crowd she
watched a lane being made by soldiers, riding before a cart.
The crowd shouted and surged after the cart, but not before
Catherine had seen three white faces staring up at her as it
were from the ground. The three priests had been bound to
one hurdle; she thought they would be attacked and trodden
to pieces as they bumped at the cart's tail over the heath,
but the next moment she saw their faces staring up at her
again from the ground. Made reckless by pity, she snatched
out the rosary beads she had carried all the way from Conster,
and held them up. No one in the crowd noticed her: they
were too busy trying to get a sight of the victims—and indeed
she could not think that the priests themselves had seen her,
though she hoped it.

The three faces disappeared again, and when she next saw
them they were upright and mounting the scaffold steps. She
could not tell which of the two strangers was Father Crockett
and which was Father James, but she at once recognized
Father Edwards. Her eyesight was keen, and even from where
she had stationed herself she could see how pale and wan and
thin he looked—as he had looked at Fuggesbroke, half in a

decline. Poor soul! she thought—he seemed dazed and bewildered, as well he might be, having been brought so suddenly to judgment and to death. She remembered him as having both more hope and more fear than other priests she had met.

It was not the intention of the authorities to shorten his misery by making him suffer first. He was withdrawn to the side of the scaffold while the taller of the two strangers went up the ladder. From the curses and hulloos of the crowd, Catherine understood that he was Father Crockett. At the foot of the ladder he paused, and turning round, knelt down before Father James, who gave him absolution, then in his turn absolved the other while he knelt. All the time Catherine was holding up her beads for them to see; owing to the slope of the ground as well as to her being on horseback, she was well above the heads of the crowd, and there was more than a chance that this honest man would see her and know that in all that mob he had a friend who prayed for him.

The crowd was more hostile than she had expected, in view of what she had been told of the Catholics around Chichester. If there were Catholics present they held their peace, as no doubt was wise of them. There was a chorus of yells, hoots and hulloos when the priest, turning again at the top of the ladder, lifted his hand to bless them. "We'll have no blessing from a traitor"—"Traitor! Traitor!" "Poisoner!" "To hell with him quick before he can do us harm." Catherine saw a woman make the sign against the evil eye. Her heart leaped as under a shock. It almost seemed as if Nicholas Pecksall had been right when he said the common folk were now all set against the true religion.

There was another shout of rage when Father Crockett began a prayer in Latin. "Hold your peace!" "Cut out his tongue!" "Mumpsimus! Mumpsimus!" yelled the crowd, and in the midst of their clamour the priest was turned off.

Then silence fell: the executioner stood on the ladder watching the victim's struggles, and when they seemed to decrease gave the order for him to be cut down. He was caught as he fell, and his clothes torn off him, so that castration and dismemberment could follow while he was still alive. Catherine had never before seen an execution for high treason, and an ordinary hanging had always stopped short of this. She began to feel a little sick, and would have closed her eyes had she been able, but a kind of paralysis had taken her, and she could not move; she could only sit there staring and holding up her beads.

She could see that Father Crockett was moving—his hands and his feet, and his head on his half-dislocated neck. She told herself that he must be unconscious, but had scarcely found comfort in the thought than a great yell came from the crowd and she saw that he was standing up, waving his arms and crying out something. He was immediately overpowered and flung down, but not before Catherine had seen his terrible blackened face. All this time Father James had not moved, save to make the sign of the Cross over him when he began to struggle. At Father Edwards she dared not look.

She was praying now out loud: she did not care who heard her. The *De Profundis* and the *Dirige* flowed from her lips in a jumbled stream. Luckily she was quite a yard or two from the edge of the crowd constricted round the scaffold, and they were all too intent on what was doing there to notice her Latin. The wind blew from the scaffold, and soon there was a stink of scorching flesh. It seemed in some horrible way to intoxicate the crowd as it blew over them, for their roar swelled into a sound that was almost a chant. "Meat!" they chanted. "Meat! Meat!"

At last the quartering was over, and Father James's turn had come. He went up to the ladder, and commended his soul to God. When they heard the English tongue there was an approving shout from the spectators. "'At, that's right!" "'At, that's an Englishman!" But he did not seem to care for their approval, and having commended his soul, he said his last prayers in Latin, whereat the clamour and racket broke out again—"Mumpsimus! Mumpsimus!"

He was turned off and cut down, and Catherine watched in terror lest he too should rise. But he did not, and what with the numbers on the scaffold and the smoke of the boiling tar she could not see what was happening. But soon she saw all too well—when the executioners turned to Father Edwards and led him forward. She could see his white face only too clearly; it seemed to her like the face of a scared child. His eyes were starting, and gazed out over the crowd as if he sought a friend. Catherine waved her arm and felt sure that he must see her, for his eyes rested on her for a moment; but the next they moved away, still seeking. Then she saw that a man in the crowd near the scaffold had lifted up his hand; Francis Edwards seemed to stare at him and the man picked off and twirled his hat. But the priest suddenly looked away as the executioner, all bloody and tarry, laid hands on him. The next moment he crumpled up and fell on his knees, screaming for mercy.

"Oh, Lord!" cried Catherine. "Oh, dear, dear Lord!" A great yell broke from the crowd, and she expected to see the wretched man carried up the ladder and flung off in a bundle. But the next moment she saw that something else was happening. Three men in black who had been standing with the magistrates on the scaffold now came forward, and she guessed that they were the Protestant ministers. They gathered round Francis Edwards, who was vomiting. She knew that they were offering him his life at a price which in his terror and exhaustion he might pay. *De profundus clamavi ad te, Domine: Domine, exaudi vocem meum.* Oh, Lord, help him; oh, Lord, spare him. . . . Oh, Lord, let him fall down dead rather than deny his faith. . . . Oh, Lord, spare him. . . . *Domine, Domine, exaudi vocem meum.* The crowd was shouting and muttering—some were urging the martyr to change his faith and save his life. " 'At, that's right—'at, that's right!" "Be a Protestant and live!" But others said: "You can never trust a Jesuit." "Set him free and he poisons us all." The cries swelled to a roar, and all the time a voice was shouting in her ear *miserere mei! miserere mei!* She did not know it was her own.

At last it seemed that the wretched priest had surrendered. He was led off by the ministers to the side of the scaffold, and a conversation took place between him and the sheriff and justices. All the time the crowd roared. On the whole it did not seem pleased at the turn affairs were taking, and the cries of " 'At, that's right!" grew fewer. The greater number seemed either sorry that they were to lose a further spectacle, or else suspicious of having an ex-priest loosed among them— "He's only saying it to save his life—his heart's still full of wickedness—he's still the servant of the Pope." Oh, Lord, help him; Lord, give him strength—let him keep his crown! But she saw a gaoler called forward to strike off his irons, and he was led stumbling to the scaffold steps.

She could stay no longer; the sheriff came to the edge of the scaffold to address the crowd, but she would not wait. She had seen enough—too much; and in that distracted moment she did not know which was too much—the sufferings of the martyrs or the sparing of the apostate. Francis Edwards had been spared—he would not have to climb that ladder, to endure that agony, to suffer that outrageous death. She was glad —she was glad. No, no—she was not glad. She was sorry. Oh, Lord, I am sorry—sorry. *Miserere mei, miserere mei.* She backed her horse out through the sallows and alders into the water-meadow. The priest could become a pedlar now—a real pedlar, not a sham one—peddling ribbons and laces and combs and scents instead of the graces of Calvary. *Miserere mei. Miserere mei.*

7

"Sir, you speak Latin!"

She started at the voice that suddenly came from beside her, and looking down saw a man running at her stirrup. She had been skirting the great water-meadow, along the brook, and her horse had been picking his way slowly through the tall grass, but when she saw the stranger she struck Ball with her whip, and he would have bounded forward had not his rein been seized by a sunburnt, powerful hand.

"Go not without hearing me. I haven't followed you for nothing."

She wondered if he were a cutpurse, and put her hand on the dagger in her belt. But his face was kindly and his dress neat and respectable.

"What do you want?" she asked him.

"Only to ask if you are a Catholic."

"Why should you think I am?"

"Because of that," and he pointed to her wrist.

To her dismay she saw that she still carried her rosary in her hand.

She turned pale, but his laugh reassured her.

"You needn't fear—I am no spy," and he plucked a chaplet out of his own bosom.

"Oh, Sir—Oh, Sir—" She gazed at him in delight, till it struck her that this might be a trap. She had heard of such things. "But why should you follow me?" she asked. "Whence come you?"

"I was in the crowd standing near the scaffold, and once or twice I looked round and saw you there on your horse, holding up your chaplet for our martyrs to see. When the end came, and you rode away, I contrived to escape out of the crowd and follow you, for I knew you must be a Catholic, and I thought you might be a friend of one of the Fathers."

"I never saw Father James or Father Crockett in my life, and I only once saw Father Edwards."

"Maybe you wish you hadn't seen him again."

"It was terrible," she said in a low voice.

"Satan hath still his kingdom, and such things have happened before, though rarely."

Catherine murmured: "He was frailer than the others."

"How mean you—in body or in soul?"

"I was thinking of his body."

He gazed at her searchingly, and she saw that his eyes were piercing and blue—like a sailor's. Then she realized that something about him was familiar. It was his hat. He had a black, steeple-crowned hat with a crimson band, and she was sure now that he was the man whom she had seen twirl his hat at Father Edwards.

"Tell me," she said. "Did you not give him a sign?"

"I would have, but he had lost all virtue and command. He saw me not, though he knew I was to be there."

Catherine now no longer suspected any trap.

"And did you follow me because you thought maybe I knew him?"

"In part; but in chief because I was surprised to see a Catholic youth alone on the edge of the crowd, and so bold as to dangle his chaplet before three hundred angry Protestants. Tell me, do you live near? Do you come of a Catholic family?"

She shook her head, not knowing for the moment what to answer him. He was still gazing at her intently, and when she did not reply he said:

"Know you by chance a young man called Simon Alard?"

Catherine turned crimson.

"Why do you ask?"

"Because you are as like as two lambs—you have the same

136

features and complexion. I could now imagine myself looking into his eyes; so I should not marvel if you were related."

"Then you know him. . . . Oh, Sir, tell me—have you seen him lately?"

"As lately as this morning."

Catherine gaped at him. She began to tremble.

"Oh, Sir, Sir—tell me where he is. He must be in England—tell me where I can—where he is."

"Till a few minutes ago I thought he was on the edge of the crowd watching the executions. That was the reason why I followed you. You are so like him that I thought it was he who sat on horseback, holding up his beads. And yet I could not understand two things—how he had come by a horse, and why he had taken leave of his senses."

"Pray, Sir, a-done with your play; and tell me where he is."

"I believe him to be at this moment in Chichester—though whereabouts in the city I cannot say. But I am to meet him at an appointed place and time, so if you are, as you look, his twin brother . . ."

"I'll come with you—you mun let me come with you. I mun see him. I was on my way to find him. When I'd seen the hanging I was riding to the harbour, to attend his ship. . . . But now he's here, already landed. . . . Thank God! Thank God! This pays for all. Thank God, indeed! I never thought to find him so quick."

The words poured out of her and she had some to-do to stop herself from crying. The stranger looked at her kindly.

"Then if you have no other business, you had better come with me to the village called Halfnakede where I am to meet him in two hours' time."

"I've no other business. . . . Anyway—oh, let me come, Sir. Is it far?"

"Two or three miles. If you will allow me, we will ride together. I am a trifle heavy on your horse's crupper, but maybe you will let me take the reins."

Catherine felt in a dream when a few moments later they rode off, he in the saddle, she on the pillion, picking their way through the long grass towards another road which he said would bring them to Halfnakede without first taking them back into Chichester. It seemed a dream that she should be riding to meet Simon, the brother whom up to ten minutes

137

ago she had thought in another country. Once or twice she told herself that it was indeed a dream, that she was not riding to meet her brother, that this man was a Protestant spy who had seen her chaplet and suspected her of complicity in some Popish plot; or else that he was a ruffian who was taking her away to some secret place to rob and murder her. . . . But she did not really believe these things. His look and manner had reassured her completely. There was something about him that gave her the same feeling of peace and confidence that she used to have with Richard Tuktone.

"Tell me," she said. "Have you heard of Squire Richard Tuktone?"

"Aye, indeed. We heard of him as soon as we landed. He is gone to receive the reward that we all hope for."

"I knew him well, and loved him," she murmured. "He loved me too, but his household loved me not. They thought me dangerous."

"And so you are—waving your chaplet before a Protestant mob. I trust your brother is being more advised."

"I said not he was my brother."

"But he is your brother—your twin brother, an't he?"

"Yes."

"Though he hath told me many times he hath no brother —but a twin sister whom he loves dearly."

Catherine bent her crimson face till her head touched his shoulder. He did not speak or move, but she seemed to know that he was smiling.

"Tell me," he said, as she kept silent. "Can he have been mistaken?"

"You—you," she said in a small voice, "you must have mistook him, Sir."

"Oh, no, I think not. He hath often spoken to me of his sister. Catherine her name is, and she is the likeness of himself. When his father conformed, he and she stood firmly by their faith, and though he hath been away from her five years he knows that she still stands firm. That's true, an't it—Catherine?"

"Sir, you confound me. Am I so poorly disguised?"

"No, you are not, and I should have suspected nothing, had I not first taken you for your brother. Then when I came up with you and found out my mistake, I would have sworn you were his twin brother had I not known he had none. At the same time you dropped me a hint that you were a girl."

"What hint?"

"When you spoke of Francis Edwards, and were pitying him because his body was frail. I said to myself, 'That is a girl's pity.' And after that I watched you closely and soon made sure, apart from what you yourself chose to tell me."

"I thought it best to dress as a man, seeing as I had to ride alone so far. I'm wearing my brother's clothes."

"He will have the start of his life when he sees you. We will give him a surprise. But tell me, why have you ridden so far to find him? What made you leave your home and family?"

Catherine faltered.

"I'd sooner not say—leastways, I'd sooner tell him first."

Her companion pressed her no further, and soon they were riding up into the village of Halfnakede.

8

They went straight to the inn, where to Catherine's surprise the host seemed to be expecting them, and showed them at once into a private room.

"Master Philips will arrive in an hour or so," said the stranger. "When he comes you may tell him that his twin brother is here."

As soon as the man was gone, he said to Catherine: "You must remember your brother is James Philips; and you—I think you must be John Philips. James and John were two mighty apostolic brethren."

"And what is your name, Sir?"

"Peter Smith. That is, 'tis as much my name as yours is John Philips."

"But your true name?"

"You had better not know. Secrets are sometimes painful to keep."

Catherine said no more, but looked about her. The table in the middle of the room was laid for a meal, with cold pies and bread and cheese and ale. She had eaten nothing that day, and as she gazed at the tempting food her mouth watered. Peter Smith must have read her looks, for he said:

"Let us sit. We shall not tarry for your brother."

He began to pour her out some ale, then stopped himself with:

"I mustn't wait on you, for it would rouse suspicion if a man of my years were seen waiting on a young boy. We fugitives have learned the wisdom of acting in private as we would in public, so help yourself to ale, my lad."

Catherine grinned and did so. Somehow she was pleased to be treated as a boy.

"Tell me," she said, "did you travel all the way from Rome with my brother?"

"All the way. This isn't the first time I've been on the English Mission, so it was thought well that I should company the young priest on his first apostolic course."

"How long is it since you left Rome?"

"A trifle less than two months. We landed at Littlehampton yesterday, and would have ridden straight to West Rooting, had we not heard that three priests were to be martyred this morning."

"Why came not Simon with you to the hanging?"

"Because at the same time we heard of it we were told of a Catholic dying in the gaol, so your brother went to anoint him."

"But there is plague in the gaol!" cried Catherine, moved by a new fear for Simon.

"Nay, 'tis only the sweat, and the sweat is all over the city. And, plague or sweat, a Catholic must be anointed when he dies, though this fellow is not in gaol for his faith, but a common prisoner."

"And my brother's with him now?"

"I trust he is, or hath only just left him. When we heard the news we settled between us that your brother should go to the gaol and try to get in; I won't say how, for as I've told you, secrets can sometimes be as sore and dangerous to life as any plague swelling. Meanwhile I was to go to Broyle Heath, and shrive Francis Edwards when his turn came."

"That was why you signalled to him."

"I gave him the sign we had agreed, but he wouldn't see me. Satan had already gotten him big with the spirit of Judas."

"Oh, never say it!" cried Catherine; "never say it."

But the sunburnt stranger would not be merciful.

140

"He was called like Judas into the company of the apostles, and like Judas he refused to be baptized with the baptism of his Master, but sold Him instead—this time for the base metal of his own miserable life. *Judas, mercator pessimus.* . . . Maybe Judas was a little undersized man with a cough. But let's not trouble with him more. I think I hear your brother's footsteps on the stairs."

9

Catherine stood up, and the next minute two identical young men faced each other. One had his hair cropped close, while the other's hung about his ears in the country style; one had a dark chin, while the other was beardless; otherwise there was little to choose between them. For a moment both felt as if they gazed into a mirror.

"Simon!" cried Catherine.

"Kate! Kate!—no, how can it be Kate?"

"'Tis Kate!" she cried, flinging her arms round him. "Surelye 'tis Kate, dressed in your clothes and come to find you!"

"But how knew you I was here?"

"I knew it not, but I've found you none the less," and the tears began to pour down her face, washing her into a woman. He held her to him and kissed her. Peter Smith stood by the window and looked out of it.

Delight, surprise, thankfulness and bewilderment made them both dumb for a while. They could only sit at the table and clasp each other's hands, seeking from the contact of flesh and blood the assurance that they were not in a dream. After a time Smith came from the window and told Simon how he had found Catherine on the edge of the crowd at the Broyle. But the young man hardly listened. He would have accepted a tale of her having fallen down out of the sky. Whichever way she had come, it was God's providence and a holy sign.

"I wondered how I should ever contrive to see you—if there were a chance of my riding from West Rooting. . . . I couldn't feel sure, even hopeful, that my letter would reach you. So I prayed—oh, dear Kate, how I have prayed and prayed!"

She noticed a change in his speech. It was more elegant and had lost the country flavour that it used to have—perhaps there was a slight foreign ring about it.

"If I hadn't met you here," she said, "I should have waited at the port till your ship came in."

"I am glad you did not have to wait. There is sweat and fever in the port even more than in the city. Besides, how would you have fared alone in such company as you would have met there? I cannot believe but that some lewd fellow would have read your disguise. . . . Tell me, Sister, how is it that you came to leave Conster and our parents. What will they say to this?"

Catherine looked him keenly in the eyes. It was a look he remembered from the old days when, always together, they found it as easy to talk with looks as with words. It meant that she had bad news to tell.

"My father is dead."

He crossed himself, but did not flinch. She noted that since his leaving her he had become a stronger soul.

"Was he reconciled to the Church before he died?"

"Alack! no."

"You shall tell me more when we're alone. But my mother, Kate?—how is she?—and how can you have the heart to leave her?"

"Reckon we'll have to be alone before I tell you that."

Peter Smith saw the hint but would not take it.

"I will leave you alone when I've had your brother's news. I would know how he fared in the prison."

"I found two thieves doomed to hang to-morrow, but like to cheat the gallows by dying of their own ills."

"They were Catholics?"

"Aye, though their faith was rusty for want of use. However, I shrove and anointed them both, and now they care not how they die."

"I only pray," said Catherine, "that you may not die of going into such places."

"I am sure to die one way or another before long—if not of any sickness, then of a public execution. Either way I die according to God's will, so there is no great matter. Tell me, Smith, what happened at the Broyle? I met some of the crowd coming back, and heard that only two martyrs suffered. Is it true that Edwards is runagate?"

"It is true, God help him!" and Smith gave an account of what had happened on the scaffold, ending with: "Your sister won't have him called Judas, but I tell her he hath sold his Lord like a wicked trader."

"It had been good for that man if he had not been born," said Simon solemnly. "Though, unlike Judas, he still hath a place for repentance, if he can find it."

"He an't the only one who's failed," said Catherine. "There's Father Oven who failed at the trial, with far less to tempt and scare him."

"Satan hath certainly been running to and fro in these last days; but now we have two martyrs more in heaven to pray for us, and by that much his reign is shortened."

Catherine wished that the unknown priest would go, and leave her alone with Simon; but he had several matters to settle first, and nearly half an hour passed before he picked up his cloak and hat.

"I'll be back at nightfall," he said, "and I'll bring horses for us both."

"What! Are you leaving here so soon?" cried Catherine.

"We never stay anywhere long, and we've already been in these parts longer than we meant. You will have a full three hours with your brother."

Catherine said nothing, but she felt sick, and when the door had shut behind him, she began to weep.

"Simon, what can I do if you leave me? Where can I go? Can't I go with you?"

"Dearest Kate, now you've found me, surely you'll go home."

"Home? I'm never going home any more. I've no home to go to."

10

She sobbed so bitterly that at first he found it hard to gather from her broken sentences exactly what had happened. He held her in his arms and tried to comfort her. At first she knew he did not understand; then she felt his body stiffen— he had got her meaning. He knew now why she could not go back to Conster or follow her mother into Essex.

She had given him only a bare and blurred account—she forgot some essential pieces of outline, she put in one or two hazy and irrelevant details. Yet she had made him see a dark, crowded room, lit only by a candle held aloft and wavering, where two men fought among the furniture—an adulterer, a cuckold, and an adulteress—his cousin, his father and his mother. Catherine made him see the dreadful sight and the still more dreadful darkness that ended it. "And Madge Piers took my mother away, and Robert Douce made me drink a glass of wine. Madge said it was my mother's stars."

"Who is Robert Douce?—and was my father dead then?"

He had to question her to get the truth, to see the tragedy in a better connection than a set of jumbled and half-finished scenes. But it was all too clear in the end. His home which he had dreamed of so often while he was away, forgetting all he had suffered there, had become a house of shame and emptiness and would soon be a house of strangers. "My inheritance hath become unto me as a lion in the wood."

"My Uncle Thomas Alard is the heir, seeing that I'm disinherited by penalties of præmunire. No doubt he will soon be at Conster."

"He was sent for, and my mother had planned to be gone before he came."

"Oh, my poor mother . . ."

"Madge says it is her stars. At her present age her planets are combust."

"It is a foul superstition! I grieve that you should hold it."

Misery had moved him to anger, but the next moment he was moved to pity, both by her suffering look, and by the realization that during all these years, while he had been living in spiritual luxury in the heart of the Church, her soul had starved on the barest means of grace. A starved soul will bring up superstition as a starved body will bring up wind—he had been cruel to blame her.

"My poor sweet Kate, you must forgive me. I shouldn't have spoken in such a way—for I can guess all that you've suffered in these last years for lack of religion."

"We had a little religion sometimes. There was Mass every now and again at Fuggesbroke. . . . But now 'tis all laid waste,"—and her tears began to fall again.

"Oh, that I could take you to Rome!" cried Simon, "and have you see the Roman religion. How you would delight in the churches, and in the ceremonies!" He realized with pity that she had never been inside a Catholic church, that she had never heard Mass except in darkness and haste and fear, that she knew nothing of the beauty of Catholic ritual, nor the fellowship of large crowds, nor the power of great leaders.

"You should see the new basilica that is to stand on the site of old St. Peter's—it will be the wonder of the world when it is done. And besides, there are all the churches that have been built over the tombs of the martyrs or over the ruins of heathen temples. You should hear the music and the singing, and see the clouds of incense go up to heaven——"

"I should like to see incense burned," said Catherine, "and smell it. Is it a very holy smell?"

"It is a smell of spices and very sweet. Sister, I'm grieved that I should have enjoyed all these things without you."

"But I too have seen beautiful things—you mun't think otherwise. Squire Tuktone had a wunnerful silver cup set with jewels, and Mistress Tuktone had just finished broidering a cloth of gold to lie over the altar, and there was a chasuble of crimson samite. . . . But now 'tis all spoiled and plundered."

He took her hand and kissed it.

"I doubt not that in God's sight it was—yea, is still—lovelier than all the jewels in the Pope's crown. It is but that I feel you have been fasting while I lived in plenty."

"I shouldn't envy you your plenty if I thought there was a chance of my ever hearing Mass again. But 'tis more than a year since I heard Mass or was shriven."

"Now you're with two priests you may surely be shriven. As for the Mass . . . I wish I could take you with us to West Rooting."

"Will there be Mass there?"

"Surely. Smith and I will be the guests of Lady Beynton, and Mass will be said at least once where it hath been said many times before."

"But may I not come with you? I shan't be any danger—and where am I to ride if I don't ride with you?"

"I must leave you some time, Kate. You can't travel far with a Priest on the English Mission."

"I can travel as far as West Rooting. Then we can think of what's to come."

"I'll ask Smith. I must be guided by him, since he was sent over with me to help my inexperience. But never fear, Kate, I won't forsake you. I'm always your brother."

After that they talked no more of religion, nor of their broken home, but of the old days together, reviving memories of Medyrsham and Wogenmarye, of adventures in the forest, of dancing round St. John's fire on the green, of snapdragon and chop-cherry in the Christmas hall. Sitting hand in hand, they could be children together, and live in a past when parents were alive and kind, and religion a simple adventure. It was not till an hour had passed that Simon unwittingly revived some of the present's pain.

"That is ever how I've thought of you, Kate, while I've been away—as a little girl with long legs, who would roll down a bank or climb a tree as readily as I would. Now and again I'd have to tell myself you were a grown woman and most likely married. Why are you not married, Kate?"

He was sorry he had asked her when he saw her face.

"Because I'm a Catholic, for one reason. . . . My father hath once or twice asked me to marry a Protestant, but I wouldn't have him, and of late years nobody hath courted me, though I shall have money if I marry."

"And if you don't?"

" 'Tis my mother's till her death."

"Have you ever thought of entering a nunnery?"

"There an't no nunnery for me to enter—leastways not in England; and anyways I'd break my heart."

"Surely not that, my dear. You love religion, and if you entered some convent abroad, in France or in Flanders, as so many Englishwomen have done lately, you would breathe a religious air and enjoy the substance of the shadow you've followed so long."

"There's no use my entering a convent while I still want to be married. . . . Besides, who'd give me a dowry? Even my mother's money won't come to me if I'm in a nunnery. Howsumever, let's not talk of that."

They talked of other things till Peter Smith's return. He brought horses for himself and Simon and asked if he was ready to start at once. To Catherine's intense joy, he made no objection to her plan of riding with them; on the contrary, he seemed to favour it.

" 'Twill look only natural to the people of this inn if the

twin brothers set out together; and should there happen to be any report of two strange priests in Chichester, the number three is all to our advantage."

"Will Lady Beynton be willing to receive Catherine?"

"No doubt she'll be willing, and happily she will be so good as to help her finish her journey. We shall not be able to ride with her farther than West Rooting."

Catherine looked at Simon, but he said nothing, so she decided to let the matter drop for the present.

Her horse was sent for, and a few minutes later they rode out all three together from the village of Halfnakede.

12

It was dusk when they set out, and the plan was that they should ride all night and come to West Rooting in the morning. Behind them from the sea a brownish fog was creeping up to Chichester, running out along the channels of the dykes to smother the city. Over her shoulder Catherine could see the Cathedral spire standing like a ghost in the twilight. The city looked small, contracted, at the foot of it.

She was glad to be riding away, though she had found her visit fruitful beyond her hopes. Some of the fruit had been bitter—she would never lose the sickness of gallows' memories or the bitter taste of Francis Edwards' apostasy; but some had been the healing, national fruit of the tree of life, fruit of the Cross—she had seen martyrs die. And the sweetest fruit she had been allowed to carry with her . . . Every time she looked at Simon riding at her side she said in her heart: It is God's Providence—thanks be to God!

The sky darkened quickly, and the stars shone out, making a thin misty dazzle behind the dark shapes of the hills. Though she had scarcely slept the night before, and had lived through a stirring and exhausting day, she did not feel tired at all. The coolness and darkness of the night seemed to sustain her, and it was a relief to find herself once again in motion. Movement brought her that rest which it always brought, and seemed to set a continuity upon it—an eternity.

If she did not feel tired, neither did she feel afraid of robbers or of ghosts. The thought of the first had never seriously alarmed her, while from the second she felt guarded by the presence of these two strong souls who did not dread them and had power over them. She and her brother rode side by side along the narrow lane, with Peter Smith leading the way a little ahead. It was almost as good as being alone with Simon. The darkness seemed to wrap them together.

They still had much to say to each other, and this time she wanted to hear his story, and all that had happened to him since he had left Conster five years ago. He told her about the English College in Rome, which from having been a hospice for pilgrims had now been turned into a seminary for priests. He told her about its first struggles and the difficulties there had been before the Jesuits took command of it. He told her about the Rector, Father Persons, with his undaunted love and zeal, and about his fellow students, many of whom were already martyrs—the latest being Father Edward James that day at Chichester. All the students were pledged to martyrdom, to bring back the Faith to England at the cost of their lives. Simon himself was pledged to it, and Catherine shuddered, though he was so used to the idea that he took it almost lightly.

Almost directly after receiving Holy Orders, he had been given his faculties and had left Rome with Peter Smith (whom he once forgetfully spoke of as Edward Amyas), and two other priests who were now in Hampshire . . . They had been more than a month travelling through France, which Simon described as a sad country, full of wars. He found the French hard and sad after the cheerful, warmhearted Italians; and the inroads of Protestantism were terrible, and were affecting the spirit of the country, even among the Catholics, turning it to thoughts of material prosperity and industrial gain.

"'Tis the same in our country, here," said Catherine. "Brother, would you believe it, our country-side is full of French Protestants, plying their trades in the midst of us and making themselves rich at our expense. There's Robert Douce, whom I told you of, who will riddle our land with iron graves, and at Rye and in those parts there's a dunnamany cloth workers and artificers, so that the burgesses are petitioning Parliament to have 'em removed. Robert Douce says 'tis because they've suffered in their own country that they come to ourn."

"No doubt they suffer, but they flourish none the less. It

148

will be a sad thing for this land when one day we discover that the Protestant religion makes us rich."

"I'd sooner we were rich ourselves than that the money went to foreigners."

Her brother sighed, and with the intuition of twinship she realized that he sighed at what she had said rather than at his own thoughts.

"Forgive me—I've offended again. But I don't understand how riches can harm a nation."

"Have you never heard of a starving man eating dirt? That's how it will be with us. We shall be starved of religion and try to fill ourselves with merchandise. I tell you it will be seven times harder to bring our country back to the Faith once she's swollen up with trade than it would be while she is still empty and feels hunger."

"Think you the true religion will soon come back?"

"Soon . . . late . . . I cannot tell, and I will not think. All I know is that it must come through blood, but not the blood of armies or armadas."

"Whose blood, then?"

"The blood of martyrs—yours and mine."

"Mine!"

"Yes, Kate—we must all shed our blood; if not in bodily drops, then in the spiritual essence of blood, which is suffering. You, my poor sweet sister, have already suffered for your faith, perhaps more than I."

"I've suffered through hunger."

"I know—and in the future you may suffer otherwise."

"Oh, Simon, I could wish to be martyred with you—I could wish us to be hanged together!"

"If it were truly to be together, and not one standing by to see the other mangled first. Think of Francis Edwards."

Catherine would not think of him.

"Please God," continued Simon, "it will not be so. He would not call upon me to abide beyond my strength, but now I cannot face the thought. Dearest Kate, I've planned another future for you, in which my courage is supported by your prayers instead of weakened by your presence."

She knew he was bringing the conversation back to the nunnery, and her spirits which had soared at the thought of martyrdom now dropped into a reluctant fear.

"Brother, you indeed wish me to go into a nunnery?"

"What else can I wish for you, Kate, if you don't marry? After all, what better can I wish for you than to become the bride of Christ?"

"But I hear no call—I—I should not like the life."

"You know not yet much of the life, and as for the call, it comes not always through inclination. There's a vocation of circumstances."

"I know—I know—but——"

"My dearest sister, you shall do nothing against your wish. 'Tis natural that finding you alone like this in the world I should be anxious to see you well provided, and maybe my natural fears may have run away with my spiritual understanding. We shan't now say another word on the matter. All I ask is that you will promise to talk it over with Lady Beynton and hear what she hath to tell you. She hath a daughter in the English Convent at Bruges."

"Well, then. I will talk to her about it."

Her heart sank lower.

13

It was quite dark all the time they rode across the downs, and sometimes they had to make their way slowly over steep, uncertain ground. They would probably have lost the track but for Peter Smith, who had already more than once made the journey from Chichester to West Rooting. The sky was black with a high mist that hid the stars. There was a smell of darkness, of night, of heaviness, and never at any time the faintest sound, except for the beating of their horses' hoofs on the turf and the murmur of their voices.

At last a pale rift showed in the east, and at the same time they came off the downs and rode through the silent village of Bury. Thence they had a well-marked road to Pulborough, where they turned into a mass of little twisting lanes, which Smith seemed to know as well as he knew the downs. The sun was rising as they came to Warminghurst, in the midst of an agricultural country, with farms and their enclosures of fields dotted about the common land. Then after Thakeham it was all forest, but a forest unthreatened by iron.

Catherine was beginning to feel tired at last, and the dawn had brought her a little chill. She found that her head ached, and that her joy in motion was growing less. She would be glad to slide from her horse's back, and to lay her head on some cool pillow. Simon, seeing that his sister was tired, suggested that they should stop at an inn and refresh themselves with a drink of ale; but Peter Smith disparaged the idea. It would be dangerous, he said, to halt at an inn they did not know, and there was no inn kept by Catholics between Half-nakede and Kent. She must take heart, for their journey's end was not far off—only a few more miles.

Catherine was ashamed to find herself defaulting now that she was in the company of heroes. She did her best to hold up her head, and listen to the tales that Smith had to tell of his adventures in England two years ago. The cool, moving leaves of the forest kept the sun from her head, and once they halted by a brook side, and all three lay down and drank deep of the cold, earth-tasting water. After that she felt better, and able to face the last three miles of her journey.

It was nearly noon when they came to the ancient clearing which hundreds of years ago the Saxons had made in the forest for their hogs. Here now was all the steading of a village—the thatched huts and cottages of the peasantry, a decent house or two, a Saxon-built church, and a little way off among the trees the roofs of a Manor.

This was Tabeler Hall, home of the Beyntons, and centre of the most important Mission in the South of England. Scarcely a priest who landed at Hulkesmouth or at Little-hampton but came to say Mass at West Rooting, and the family had enjoyed an immunity which was rare, but possible in such times of personal favour and arbitrary administration.

The Beyntons were known and beloved throughout the neighbourhood, both by the Squires and Magistrates, and by the common folk, among whom otherwise the hope of gain might have made informers. They lived with discretion, but so securely that for weeks at a time they had been able to keep the Blessed Sacrament in their home. Here at last Catherine was to find English Catholics whose faith was not starved, and she took heart again as she heard Peter Smith tell their story. It would be good to rest at Tabeler Hall, even if afterwards she must leave it, like Simon Peter, to be carried whither she would not go . . .

She was so tired that she had almost fallen asleep by the time she reached the house, and was conscious only of a hurry and stir about her as she sat nodding on her saddle. Then Simon came up, leading an elderly lady dressed in black and followed by a thick-set young man, to both of whom he introduced her as his sister. She was relieved to find that she would not have to maintain her disguise, for she had scarcely the wits for it now. Soon she found that all disguises were unneeded here, and Peter Smith and James Philips were openly Father Amyas and Father Alard.

For the first time in her life Catherine found herself in a Catholic household; from the lowest scullion to the dowager head of the family, all held the Faith and practised it according to opportunity. She dismounted stiffly from her horse, and entered the hall on her brother's arm. She was aware of many people about her—she saw two young boys kneeling to receive Father Amyas's blessing—servants came forward with trays of food and wine—she was led to a seat by the fire and found herself shivering.

"What will you take, child?" asked Lady Beynton. "Here is some lamb pasty, some soused eels, and some salad—or will you have marchpane? Ralphe, pour out some wine."

But Catherine found that she could not eat; she could only sip a little wine, and then feel glad to go upstairs, where her ladyship's own woman took her to a guest-chamber and helped her to undress. Soon she was asleep.

14

She did not sleep well. Every now and then she would wake, feeling terrified till she remembered where she was; and when at last she managed to sleep for a few hours she woke with memories of many dreams, to find her body covered with sweat that clogged her shift and the sheets.

After that she did not sleep again, but lay awake thinking. She heard a clock strike five, and thought that someone would be sure to call her soon to supper, so that it was not worth while trying to go to sleep. The sunlight came like a red sword between the heavy curtains. She watched it move across the room till it lay upon her bed; then it moved till it touched her heart—it looked as if the sunset pierced her with a sword. The sun was a jealous lover, running her through the heart, because she was going to leave him, to shut herself out of his power, though surely the sun would not be quite shut out of the cloisters at Bruges . . . No, but he would touch her only respectfully, his kisses would never again burn her face and neck as brown as a field of hay; she would grow pale as hemlock . . . She had never seen a nun, but she knew that nuns were pale.

"Then, O, then, O, then, O, my true love said:
Till this time come again I cannot live a maid . . ."

No, I cannot, I cannot, I cannot—but I must. I am condemned to an eternal maidenhood . . . I who want love, even Protestant love . . . No, no, no, I do not—not now. He was terrible—he killed both my father and my mother. Oh, what am I thinking . . . ?

Her head was hot and swimming with thoughts, and she raised herself on her pillows that she might clear them. This nunnery—she would have to face it. If she would not go into a nunnery, where else could she go? Could she go back to Conster and live with her uncle? She would live in shame and dependence because all her uncle's family would know why she did not live with her mother. Could she live with her mother? No, she could never do that. Could she live with Simon? No, for he would have no home and probably soon would lose his life as well. Oh, Simon, Simon . . . tears oozed from under her eyelids, and seemed to dry at once on her hot cheeks. Why couldn't she and Simon live together as brothers and sisters do? Why must religion take him from her to wander about the world until he left it? When a woman does not marry . . . Oh, why couldn't she marry? Why must religion make it impossible for her to find a mate? Religion had breathed over her like a hot wind from the desert, withering up its flower.

She must not think such thoughts. They were wicked and blasphemous. A demon was surely whispering to her—*libera nos a malo*. The Lord is my firmament, my God is my helper. I would die for my religion. She thought of how she had wanted to die with Simon, feeling that she could even bear to see him mangled if they might share the joy of martyrdom together. Simon wanted her to go into a nunnery—he had no wish to see her with him on the scaffold, the sight of her sufferings would weaken him. If she were somewhere happy and safe he would feel stronger to die. That was why he wanted her to go into a convent—he knew she would be safe and he thought she would be happy. She would have the substance of religion—all the holy privileges she had never known: Mass even every day and constant prayer with those of her own faith. She would sit down to a banquet after years of starvation.

But banquets do not always tempt those who are used to eating under hedges. All her life she had been a gipsy in religion and now she felt herself shrinking from the thought of settled ways. It was wrong, she knew, but she could not help it. A sudden wild idea came to her to put on her man's attire again, and ride out into the country, and from henceforward be an adventurer. She would rather wear a man's doublet and side-lops than a nun's trailing robes . . . though years ago she used to think and sometimes say what a sin it was that there were no convents in England for a woman to go to . . . But she had no vocation—she wanted to be married . . . Simon said there was such a thing as a vocation of circumstances. What else could she do if she did not go into a nunnery? She could not really ride away as a man. She could not take the roads as a vagabond—not for any length of time. She had not quite the stuff in her for that.

She had told Nicholas Pecksall that her religion was the dearest thing to her in life (or she might have married a dancing Parson). Then she ought to love it better than her freedom. Religion was something more than plots and risks and contrivances. It was life and death. She wished it could be death, but it was not expedient for her to die . . . expedient, expedient—that was a word of Nicholas Pecksall's. She did not like expediency. But Simon did not wish her to die—oh, how her head ached!—he wished her to live and pray for him. By prayers and blood . . . and he had said it would not be the blood of armadas—nor only the blood of martyrs. If she poured out her soul in suffering she might bring back the Faith to England, even though she did not pour out her blood, as she would so much rather do. She mustn't weaken Simon, and the cause that was his and hers. If only her head didn't ache so, she would get this clearer. Thousands of priests, marching from Rome, from Rheims, from Douay, to be hanged in England, and a poor nun praying in Bruges who would rather be hanged—and the Faith is back again.

15

There was a knock at her door, and Lady Beynton's woman came in, carrying an armful of her mistress's clothes. Supper would be served in half an hour, she said, and she helped Catherine to dress. The clothes were stiff and rich, such as Catherine was not used to, and for the first time in her life she had to wear a ruff, instead of the parlet that had left her neck free and sunburnt. The ruff scratched her chin, and made her headache worse; but she endured it as good practice for the days when her head and neck would be bound up together in a nun's coif.

Supper was laid in the great hall, and was a well-cooked, bountiful meal eaten with solemnity. Sir Ralphe Beynton, virtual head of the house, sat at the head of the table, with his mother, the actual and effectual head, at his left hand. Catherine sat on his right, and below her and Lady Beynton came the two priests, and afterwards other members of the family, none of whom yet was married. The men and women of the household sat down with their masters. It all reminded Catherine a little of Fuggesbroke, except that the food and table furniture were of the best, and the atmosphere was both less fearful and less gay.

Catherine could eat only a little, to the concern of her hostess. She was ashamed of feeling tired and languid, but told herself she would be well again after a night's rest. Neither did she feel able to join much in the conversation, though she enjoyed listening to the tales of Rome and foreign parts. It appeared that Lady Beynton had a son in the new college at Douay as well as a daughter in the nunnery at Bruges, also that at one time she had been to Flanders to see them both. Catherine was puzzled to think how she could have contrived it.

It was not till they had left table that she heard there would be Mass the next morning. At first she thought this meant the end of her night's rest at one or two o'clock, but she was told that these things did not have to be done so desperately at Tabeler Hall. Father Amyas would say Mass at six o'clock, before setting out again on his journey. Simon, she learned to her inexpressible joy, would stay a day or two longer at West Rooting.

"Then I am to join Amyas at Rochester—and I shall travel by way of Leasan and Vinehall."

"Shall you go to Conster?"

He shook his head. "There is nothing now to take me to Conster. But I shall go to Fuggesbroke and to Holly Crouch."

"Shall you see Thomas Harman?"

"That's my chief purpose."

"To reconcile him?"

"Aye, to finish your work."

"My work?—it was none of my work—my mischief, rather." But she was comforted to hear Simon speak of the reconciliation of Thomas Harman as her work.

She was also comforted to find that her talk with Lady Beynton about the future was not to happen that night. She would far sooner go upstairs to her room and creep into bed again, though she had been out of it barely three hours. She thought now that she must have caught some kind of sickness in Chichester; for she was certain that she had a fever—her head ached and her pulses throbbed, and her skin felt hot and burning. Doubtless there were many fevers about in the city and she remembered having heard that in October the decline of the Sign of Virgo made for fevers and sweats.

All she hoped was that she would not be too sick and heavy for Mass to-morrow morning. She would have liked to ask for some remedy, such as a lavender poultice or an infusion of ragwort. But she did not want anyone to take alarm at her state and maybe forbid her to come to Mass. At all costs, in spite of herself and in spite of anyone, she would be there. The cup should not be snatched from her lips a second time.

Her resolution grew with her illness, as she lay in the great bed, sleeping lightly and fitfully, and always chased by dreams. Once she dreamed that she had overslept, that no one had waked her, that Mass was over and both the priests were gone. She set out after them—riding—riding—she would hear Mass at Fuggesbroke. She could see it far off, but she came no nearer, though she beat and urged on Ball; and then suddenly flames rose up out of the roof, and she could feel the heat of them, though they were ten miles away.

Another time she dreamed that she was riding dressed in a nun's habit. Riding in her dreams was never the rest and release it was in her waking hours, rather it was something that wore her out, that seemed part of a useless struggle . . . She was riding and she met Nicholas Pecksall, and for some reason Richard Tuktone was there too. They were in the Parsonage garden, and she could see great roses growing up a kind of frame that towered against the sky. Pecksall put his arms round her and kissed her—she could feel his kisses in her dream—and all the time Richard Tuktone stood by them and would not go. Then she woke, feeling the dream still about her, and knowing that the frame up which the roses climbed was a gallows. "Gallows-garden," she heard herself saying aloud; "Gallows-garden."

She prayed desperately, because she thought her wits were leaving her. But after a while she was able to reassure herself that it was only a dream. She was not used to illness, but she knew that in a fever dreams have a strange intensity. As soon as Mass was over she would ask for medicine.

16

Mass was over . . . or had she dreamed it? No, for she could remember it so clearly. The altar stood like an island among the mists that were gathering round her—an island that burned at each end. She could see it there even when she closed her eyes, and the household kneeling round it, and Simon standing before it, with Father Amyas at his side to serve the heavenly table. She could hear her brother's voice: *introibo ad altare Deo*. She had gone up to the altar of God after two years. That was why she did not feel afraid now, though she knew she must be very ill. She did not fear anything, even death itself, now that she was sure the Mass was not a dream. She was quite, quite sure, for she could remember how a long ray of light had slanted down from the window to touch the chalice. She could remember the colours of the clothes the family wore—black for Lady Beynton, purple for Sir Ralphe, watchet for Joyce and green for Margery . . . and she could remember how at the end of Mass she had fallen backwards against Humphrey's shoulder. That proved it. She would never have dreamed that.

But how was it that Nicholas Pecksall could have said the

Mass?—how had he managed to come as far as West Rooting? She must ask Father Amyas, for she could see his face above her, clear among the shadows. But instead she found herself telling him that the decline of the Sign of Virgo often brings fevers and sweats.

"They've sent for a physician," he said, and she was glad to find that she could hear his voice quite clearly, and that it sounded cool and rational. Her own did not seem quite so rational as she heard it say:

"It should be a conjurer, for all these things are in the stars."

"Nay, Mistress, our sicknesses have not such a dignity. Rather they come from the dust of the earth than the stars of heaven . . . The physicians of the Jesuit order . . . travelling . . . inns . . . lice and vermin . . . contagion . . . good hope . . ."

His voice seemed to come from very far away, which was strange, because his face was still quite close to hers. His voice seemed to ebb and flow like the sea waves. She suddenly felt scared, and called: "Simon! Simon!"

"I'm here."

There was a hand in hers. She held it, and clung to it.

"Where's Father Amyas?"

"He hath been gone two hours."

"Simon, you wöan't go—you wöan't leave me——"

"No, dear Kate."

She could hear voices murmuring, men's and women's, ebbing and flowing and sighing. Then she felt a prick, and a kind of languor. She could hear something being poured into a bowl.

"Simon, when you get to Holly Crouch, will you let them know at Fuggesbroke?" She was feeling much clearer, though very weak. She could see the room and the people in it without mistiness, and she could feel the bed and the pillows under her instead of floating in a treacherous void. Simon sat at the foot of the bed, watching her.

"Yes, I shall go to Fuggesbroke. Are you better now?"

"Aye, I am clearer in my head."

"The doctor hath just bled you. He took two ounces of blood from your foot."

"My feet feel cold."

158

"That is the fever leaving you."

Lady Beynton came forward with a cup of milk, but Catherine found she could take very little of it.

"How much longer will you stay here?" she asked her brother.

"I shall stay until you're better."

"Have I the sweat?"

"The physician thinks you have some sort of putrid fever. He doth not think it is the sweat."

"Then I pray none of you catches it from me. Simon, you mun take care."

"I always take care," he said, smiling at her.

Her pillow was growing hot, and she tried to turn it over, but found she was too weak. Lady Beynton turned it and Catherine's head fell back. The pillow seemed to stand out round her like a nun's coif.

17

Mass was over . . . no, she hadn't dreamed it. She could remember it so clearly. Or had she dreamed it?—for there was nothing now, only a void beneath her and above her and a great darkness. Ah, now she remembered—there was to have been Mass at Fuggesbroke, and on her way to it Thomas Harman had met her and told her that the soldiers had come and beaten up Tuktone . . . She had run away disguised as a pedlar . . . She was trying to find Simon. He was in Rome, at the English College, and she was trying to find him, though she had lost her horse and all her money, and had the plague . . . *miserere mei* . . . she was in a ship burning at both ends . . . oh, Simon! Simon! . . .

"I'm here, darling Kate. Don't you know me?"

. . . Simon by her side in the darkness, waiting for the first light, so that they could slide down the wall together and run away to Leasan . . . no, they were in the dark forest of Wogenmarye, so very dark—the trees were hiding the stars. Simon, can you see the stars? O, God my firmament . . . Go forth, Christian soul, from this world . . . Squire Tuktone said "We shall meet in Paradise" . . . Simon would die on the gallows—no, no, in the prison . . . in the name of Christ, Son of the living God who suffered for thee . . . Who's that playing a lute? I like not the music—let me go! let me go!—he

159

is treading on the lute . . . mother! mother! . . . let thine habitation to-day be in peace, and thine abode in Sion.

She was lying with her knees raised, and a crucifix was propped against them. Simon was kneeling beside her; she felt as if she had wakened between two sleeps.

"Brother, how long have I been ill?"

"Around five days."

It seemed more like five minutes—or five years.

"Then how much longer can you stay with me?"

"I shall stay as long as you need me."

"That won't be much longer now," she said, and knew that she was dying.

She was not afraid, but she would have liked to keep her head clear. She wanted to speak to Simon—to ask him to say Mass for her soul; but the words would not come. Then she knew that he would say it without her asking.

Her mind was slipping back into darkness . . . she groped for her brother's hand and touched the wood of the cross. It was time to start, or Nicholas Pecksall would have begun Mass. Why didn't they light the candles? . . . gallows-garden . . . who said that? . . . I want my horse—I want my horse . . . O, God, my firmament . . . I cannot be a nun . . . a gittern and a recorder . . . then, O, then, O, then, O, my true love said . . . may the choir of angels receive thee, and mayest thou have eternal rest with Lazarus who once was poor . . .

An altar with a candle burning at each end . . . she and Simon were kneeling before it . . . there was no darkness now . . . she could see the light, and it seemed as she watched it to increase and surge up like sunrise . . . *introibo ad altare Deo* . . . the light swept towards her and blazed about her and then became a sound . . . a Name . . . a Name that was on her lips. Then the sound once more became light and the light darkness, but a darkness without fear. She knew that she had only to look up to see the sky ablaze with stars—stars that were no longer the distant arbitrators of man's fate but the tokens of God's unchanging mercy towards him. So she closed her eyes in sleep and gave herself to the darkness.